MW01717422

"Afraid to get your hair wet?"

"I want to resemble Esther Williams, not Boy George," Elizabeth answered. He laughed and Elizabeth couldn't remember hearing a more pleasant sound. "You should laugh more often."

"Me?" A frown darkened his eyes. "You're the one who needs a few lessons on having fun." He swam to her and placed a hand around her waist. "Let's take this wave together."

Given no option, Elizabeth was thrust into the oncoming wall of water. As they went under the giant surge, she panicked, frantically lashing out with her arms and legs.

"Are you all right?" Andrew called.

"No," she screamed, coughing and choking on her words. Saltwater stung her eyes. "You did that on purpose," she accused him angrily.

"Of course I did," he countered. "It's supposed to be fun."

"Fun!" she spat. "Marie-Antoinette's walk to the guillotine was more fun than that!"

Dear Reader,

Although our culture is always changing, the desire to love and be loved is a constant in every woman's heart. Silhouette Romances reflect that desire, sweeping you away with books that will make you laugh and cry, poignant stories that will move you time and time again.

This summer we're featuring Romances with a playful twist. Remember those fun-loving heroines who always manage to get themselves into tricky predicaments? You'll enjoy reading about their escapades in Silhouette Romances by Brittany Young, Debbie Macomber, Annette Broadrick and Rita Rainville.

We're also publishing Romances by many of your all-time favorites such as Ginna Gray, Dixie Browning, Laurie Paige and Joan Hohl. Your overwhelming reaction to these authors has served as a touchstone for us, and we're pleased to bring you more books with Silhouette's distinctive medley of charm, wit and—above all—*romance*. I hope you enjoy this book, and the many stories to come.

Sincerely,

Rosalind Noonan
Senior Editor
SILHOUETTE BOOKS

SRRL-7/85

DEBBIE MACOMBER

A Friend or Two

Silhouette Romance

Published by Silhouette Books New York

America's Publisher of Contemporary Romance

SILHOUETTE BOOKS
300 E. 42nd St., New York, N.Y. 10017

Distributed by Pocket Books

ISBN: 0-373-08392-0

First Silhouette Books printing October 1985

10 9 8 7 6 5 4 3 2 1

America's Publisher of Contemporary Romance

Printed in the U.S.A.

Books by Debbie Macomber

Silhouette Special Edition

Starlight #128
Borrowed Dreams #241

Silhouette Romance

That Wintery Feeling #316
Promise Me Forever #341
Adam's Image #349
The Trouble with Caasi #379
A Friend or Two #392

DEBBIE MACOMBER

has quickly become one of Silhouette's most prolific authors. As a wife and mother of four, she not only manages to keep her family happy, but she also keeps her publisher and readers happy with each book she writes.

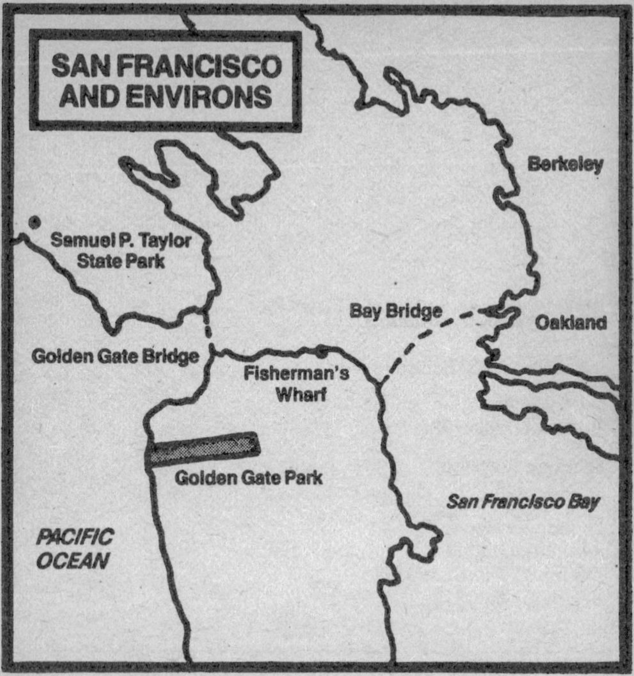
SAN FRANCISCO
AND ENVIRONS
Berkeley
Samuel P. Taylor
State Park
Bay Bridge
Oakland
Golden Gate Bridge
Fisherman's
Wharf
Golden Gate Park
San Francisco Bay
PACIFIC
OCEAN

OREGON
IDAHO
Sacramento
NEVADA
San Francisco
Fresno
CALIFORNIA
ARIZONA
Los Angeles
San Diego

Prologue

Miss Elizabeth." The elderly butler's eyes widened. He composed himself quickly. "This is a surprise. Welcome home."

"Thank you, Bently. It's good to be home." Elizabeth looked around the huge entry hall with its elegant crystal chandelier and imported rugs from the Orient and sighed inwardly. Home. Would it offer her what she hadn't been able to find in Europe? Immediately doubts filled her.

"Would you see to my luggage," Elizabeth instructed in a low, disturbed tone. "And have Helene draw my bath."

"Right away."

Removing her white gloves one finger at a time, Elizabeth looked around her with a renewed sense of appreciation for all this house represented. Wealth.

Tradition. Family pride. With all this at her fingertips, how could she possibly be dissatisfied?

"Bently, do you know where Father is?"

"In the library, miss," he responded crisply with a heavy English accent.

Elizabeth's smile was absent as she started across the huge hall. She loved Bently. Little could ruffle this refined servant; she could recall the time...Loud voices drifted from the partially opened door and caused her to pause. Her father rarely raised his voice.

"I'm afraid I've failed her, Mother. Elizabeth is restless and unhappy."

Stunned, Elizabeth stood just outside the library door.

"But, Charles, give the girl time. She's suffered a great loss." Her grandmother's raspy voice was just as troubled.

"She has no drive, no ambition, no purpose. Dear heavens, have you seen these expense reports from Paris?"

The sound of his fist against the desk shocked her.

"Elizabeth goes through money as if there was no tomorrow. I've pampered and indulged her since Mary died, and now I'm left to deal with it."

"But she's such a dear child."

"Dear, but hopelessly unhappy, I fear. The thing is"—her father's voice lowered and took on a slightly husky quality—"I don't know how to help her."

A twinge of guilt caused Elizabeth to lower her head fractionally. She'd thought she had concealed her discontent. She couldn't argue; her spending had been extravagant the last few months.

"What can we do?" Again, it was her grandmother.

"I don't know, Mother."

Elizabeth had never heard such resignation from her father. "I'll talk to her, but I don't know what good it will do. Perhaps if Mary had lived..." he continued soberly.

Elizabeth refused to listen to any more. Her father rarely spoke of her mother. Mary Elizabeth Wainwright's unexpected death two years before still had the power to inflict a deep sense of loss on them both. Elizabeth's brother had adjusted well, but he was older and far more able to cope with his grief.

Thoughtfully, Elizabeth climbed the long, winding staircase to her rooms. A confrontation with her father was the last thing she wanted. How could she explain this lackadaisical attitude that had taken over her usually cheerful existence? She had assumed that her feelings were well disguised. And as for the fruits of wealth, she was well aware of the privileges and the power. But money wasn't everything; it didn't bring happiness or fulfillment. The best time she'd had in her life had been the summer she bummed her way across France. And she'd barely had two francs to rub together. Not only was she intelligent, but she was gifted. She spoke fluent French and enough Italian and German to make her last visits to Rome and Berlin worry-free. But what good was any of this to her now?

Sitting on the plush canopy bed, Elizabeth straightened. She was a Wainwright. She was supposed to maintain her pride and independence at all times.

A gnawing ache churned her stomach. She didn't want to talk to her father. She didn't want to explain the fiasco in Paris and her extravagant expenses. All she wanted was peace and quiet. The germ of an idea began to form in her mind. Her bags were still packed. She could slip out just as noiselessly as she'd slipped in. San Francisco sounded appealing. Her mother had spent a carefree summer there when she was about Elizabeth's age. With a renewed sense of purpose, she slipped out the bedroom door and down the back stairs.

Chapter One

The ever-present odor of fresh fish and the tangy scent of salt water followed Elizabeth as she sauntered down Fisherman's Wharf. The wharf wasn't far from where she was staying at the St. Francis, one of San Francisco's most prestigious hotels. A little breeze ruffled her golden-brown hair and added a shade of color to her otherwise palc features.

With the morning paper clenched under her arm, Elizabeth strolled into a small French café. It had only taken three days for the restless, bored spirit to make its way into her thoughts. How could she sit in one of the most beautiful cities in the world with the homey scent of freshly baked bread drifting from the restaurant kitchen and feel this listlessness?

A friendly waitress dressed in a crisp pink uniform with a starched white apron took Elizabeth's order for coffee and a croissant. She wasn't hungry but had noticed this morning the way her clothes were beginning to hang on her and decided to make the effort to eat something.

Lackadaisically her eye ran over the front page of the newspaper. Nothing had changed. The depressing stories of war and hate were the same on this day as they had been the week and the month before that. Sighing, she folded the newspaper and waited for the waitress to bring her the coffee and roll.

"Are you looking for a job?" The young waitress's eyes rounded eagerly as she delivered the order to Elizabeth.

"I beg your pardon?"

"I saw you looking through the paper and thought you might be job-hunting. I wouldn't normally suggest something like this, but there's a job here and now if you'd like."

Elizabeth's pale blue eyes widened incredulously. What was this girl talking about?

"I know it's not much, but a position here could tide you over until you find what you're really looking for. The other girl who normally works with me called in this morning and quit." She paused to forcefully release her breath. "Can you imagine? Without a minute's notice. Now I'm left to deal with a lunch crowd all by myself."

Elizabeth straightened in the chair. Why not? She didn't have anything better to do. "I don't know that I'd be much help. I've never been a waitress."

"It doesn't matter." The younger girl's relief was obvious. "I can guarantee that by the end of the day you'll discover everything you ever cared to know about waitressing and a few things you didn't." Her laugh was light and cheerful. "By the way, I'm Gilly. Short for Gillian."

"And I'm Elizabeth."

"Glad to meet you, Elizabeth. Boy, am I glad." The breezy laugh returned. "Come on back to the kitchen, and I'll introduce you to Evelyn. He's the owner and chef." With determined, quick-paced steps, Gilly led the way across the room to the swinging double doors. She paused and turned around. "Don't be shocked if Evelyn kisses you or something. The French sometimes do that."

"I won't be surprised." Elizabeth murmured and had trouble containing her smile, wondering what Gilly would say if she knew that Elizabeth spoke the language fluently and had lived in Paris.

A variety of pleasant smells assaulted her as she entered the spotless kitchen. As a little girl her favorite place in the huge, rambling house had been the kitchen. The old cook would often sneak her pieces of pie dough or a cookie. Elizabeth's childhood had been happy and untroubled.

"Evelyn," Gilly said, attracting the attention of the chef who was garbed completely in white and working busily at the stove. "This is Elizabeth. She's going to take Deanne's place."

The ruddy-faced man with a thick mustache that was shaped like an open umbrella over a full mouth turned and stared blankly at Elizabeth.

Giving in to an impulse, Elizabeth took a step forward and extended her hand. In flawless French, she explained that she hadn't done any waitressing but would be pleased to help them out this afternoon.

Laughing, Evelyn broke into a wild speech in his native language while pumping her hand as if she were a long lost relative.

Again in perfect French, Elizabeth announced that, no, she wasn't from France or Quebec, but had spent several years studying in his country.

An expression of astonishment widened Gilly's eyes. "You should have said you were from France."

"I'm not. I studied French in school." Elizabeth didn't explain that the school had been in Paris.

"You know, that's one thing I'm sorry for," Gilly said, thoughtfully pinching her bottom lip between two fingers. "I wish I'd studied French. A lot of good Spanish does me now. But then"—she paused and chuckled—"I could always end up working in a Mexican restaurant."

Elizabeth laughed. Gilly was delightful. Amiable and full of enthusiasm, the younger girl was just the antidote Elizabeth needed for the long, boring day that lay before her.

Luckily, the two were close enough in size that Elizabeth could wear one of Gilly's extra uniforms.

After a minimum of instruction, Elizabeth was given a pad and pencil and asked to wait on her first customers, an elderly couple who asked for coffee and croissants. Without incident, Elizabeth delivered their order.

"This isn't so bad,' she murmured under her breath to Gilly, who was busy writing out the luncheon special on the chalkboard to display on the sidewalk.

"I took one look at you and knew you'd do great," Gilly stated cheerfully.

"You took one look at me and saw an easy mark." A smile revealed deep grooved dimples in each of Elizabeth's cheeks.

"Does everyone call you Elizabeth?" Briefly, Gilly returned her attention to the chalkboard. "You look more like a Beth to me."

Beth, Elizabeth mused thoughtfully. No one had called her that since her school days, and then only her best friends. After all, she was a Wainwright. Elizabeth was the dignified name her family preferred.

"Call me anything you like," she said in a teasing tone. "No, on second thought, you better stick with Beth."

A half-hour later, Elizabeth was answering to a variety of names, among them "Miss" and "Waitress." Never had she imagined that such a simple job could be so demanding or that there were so many things to remember. The easy acceptance given her by the customers was a pleasant surprise. Most of the café's luncheon crowd were regulars from office buildings close to the wharf. Several of the regulars paused to chat with Elizabeth before ordering. A couple of men blatantly flirted with her, which did wonders for her sagging ego. A few asked about Deanne, and weren't surprised when they learned that she'd quit.

The highlight of the afternoon came when Elizabeth waited on a retired couple visiting from France. She spoke to them in their native language for so long that Gilly had to point out that there were several of Elizabeth's other customers who needed attention. Later, Gilly was shocked to see that the couple had left Elizabeth a tip as large as the price of their meal.

"Tutor me in French, would you?" she joked as she passed Elizabeth, carrying a glass coffee pot.

Elizabeth couldn't believe the time when she glanced at her gold wristwatch. Four o'clock. The day had sped past, and she felt exhilarated; better than she had in months. Tonight she wouldn't need a pill to help her sleep.

"You were terrific. Everyone was saying how great you were." Gilly lavished on additional praise. "A couple of regulars said they hoped that you'd stay. And even if it was your first time waitressing, you were as good as Deanne ever was."

After all the orders she had mixed up, Elizabeth was surprised Gilly thought so. Of course, she had eaten in some of the world's best restaurants and knew what kind of service to expect. But giving it was something else entirely.

"Would you consider staying on for a while?" Gilly's enthusiastic voice was a mixture of hope and doubt. "I know this isn't the kind of job you want. But the pay isn't bad and the tips are good."

Elizabeth hesitated. "I...I don't know."

"It would only be until we could find someone to replace you," Gilly added quickly. "That shouldn't be long. A week or two. Three months at the most."

"Three months," Elizabeth gasped.

"Well, to be honest, Evelyn saw you with the French couple and told me that he'd really like to hire you permanently. I suppose it's too much to ask, with your qualifications."

What qualifications? Elizabeth mused. Oh sure, she knew all the finer points of etiquette, but aside from her skill with languages, Elizabeth had never had any formal job training.

"Just think about it, okay?" Gilly urged.

Elizabeth agreed with a soft smile.

"You'll be back tomorrow?" The doelike eyes implored, making it impossible to refuse.

Exhaling slowly, Elizabeth nodded. "Sure. Why not?"

Why not indeed, Elizabeth mused as she unlocked the door to her suite at the St. Francis. Her feet hurt and there was an ache in the small of her back, but otherwise she felt terrific.

The hot water filling the tub was steaming up the bathroom when Elizabeth straightened. There wasn't anyone she wanted to visit this summer, no place she wanted to go. There wasn't anything to stop her from working with Gilly. It'd be fun. Well, maybe not fun...but different, and she was definitely in the mood for different.

With the sound of the hot water running behind her, Elizabeth knotted the sash to her blue silk robe and eased her feet into matching slippers. Sitting atop the mattress, she reached for the phone. For the first time in months, she felt like talking to her father. He had a right to know where she was staying and what she was up to. Over the last year she'd given him enough to worry about.

The family butler answered the phone. "Good evening, Miss Elizabeth."

"Hello, Bently. Is my father home?"

"I'll get him for you."

Had she detected a note of worry in the butler's tone? With Bently it was difficult to discern any emotion.

"Elizabeth dear." Her father spoke crisply. "Just exactly where are you?" He didn't wait for her to answer. "Bently said that you were home, and before anyone knew what had happened you were off again."

"I'm sorry, Dad," she stated, happily proving that she wasn't the least bit regretful. "I'm in San Francisco. I've got a job."

"A job," her father repeated in a low, shocked tone. "Doing what?"

Elizabeth laughed, mentally picturing the perplexed look working its way across the grooved lines in her father's aged face. With a liberal arts degree as vague and unimpressive as her grades, Elizabeth knew her father doubted that anyone could employ her. "I'm a waitress in a small French café called The Patisserie."

"A waitress!" Charles Wainwright exploded.

"Now don't go all indignant on me. I know this is a shock. But I'm enjoying it. Some of the customers speak French, and the chef is from Paris."

"Yes, but..."

Elizabeth could feel her father's shock. "But if you wanted to work, there would be a hundred positions more suited to you."

"Honestly, Dad, I'd think you'd be happy that I was out of your hair for the summer. Wish me well and kiss Grandmother for me."

"Elizabeth..."

"My bath's running. I've got to go."

A resigned note Elizabeth recognized all too well entered his voice. "Take care of yourself, my dear."

"This is working out great," Gilly commented at the end of Elizabeth's first week. "I don't know what it is, but there's something about you that the customers like."

"It's because I can pronounce the name of Evelyn's delicate pastries," Elizabeth returned in a teasing voice.

"That's not it," Gilly contradicted with a slight quirk of her head. Short, bouncy curls bobbed with the action. "I don't know, but having you speak French adds a certain class to the place."

"My French may be good, but my feet are killing me." She faked a small, pain-filled sigh and rubbed the bottom of one loafer over the top of the other.

"Your feet wouldn't hurt if you were wearing the right kind of shoe."

Elizabeth glanced at her Guccis and groaned. Heavens, she'd spent more on these leather loafers than she made in a week at this restaurant. How could they possibly be the wrong kind of shoe?

"If you like, we can go shopping after work and I'll show you what you should be wearing."

Gilly's offer was a pleasant surprise. "Yes, I'd like that."

"It'll give me an excuse not to go home." Discontent coated Gilly's normally happy voice.

"What's the matter with home?"

One petite shoulder was raised in a halfhearted shrug. "Nothing, I guess. It's just that I turned twenty last month, and I hate living with my parents."

"So get an apartment." Elizabeth suggested the obvious, wondering why Gilly hadn't thought of that herself.

Gilly's returning smile was stiff. "So speaks the voice of inexperience. I don't suppose you've gone looking for apartments lately. Have you seen how much they want these days?" Elizabeth had continued to live at the St. Francis. The hotel was convenient and close, and what meals she didn't eat at the Patisserie were promptly delivered to her room after a simple phone call.

"It isn't that I haven't tried," Gilly continued, oblivious to Elizabeth's seeming lack of emotion. "I found a boarding house and stayed there until my mother found out about my neighbors."

"Your neighbors?"

"I admit they were a bit unusual," Gilly mumbled disparagingly. "I never saw the girl in the room next to me, but every morning there were two empty yogurt cartons outside her door."

Elizabeth couldn't restrain her soft laugh.

"That was nothing," Gilly continued, her own appealing laugh blending with Elizabeth's. "The woman on the other side of my room looked like a Russian weight lifter who has failed a hormone test. One look at her—or him, whichever the case may be—and my mother had me out of there so fast my head was spinning."

Elizabeth could sympathize with her friend. "I know what you mean. I moved away from home as soon as I could too."

"And if I left, my younger sister could have her own room and..." Gilly paused, her hand gripping Elizabeth's forearm. "He's back."

"Who?" Elizabeth glanced up to see a tall, broad-shouldered man enter the café. The first thing that impressed her was his size. He was easily six foot four. Yet he carried himself with an unconscious grace that reminded her briefly of a martial arts expert. He wasn't handsome. His jaw was too angular, too abrupt. His mouth was firm, and even from this distance she noticed that it was slightly compressed, as if something had displeased him.

"Him," Gilly whispered under her breath. "How long has it been since you've seen such an unqualified stud?"

"Obviously too long," Elizabeth responded, picking up a menu and water glass. "But then, isn't one stud just like another?" she asked blandly. Although not strikingly handsome, this man was compelling enough to attract the women's attention.

"One stud just like another?" Gilly repeated on a low, disbelieving breath. "Beth, if you consider his type a stud, then this guy is Secretariat."

Elizabeth had difficulty hiding her smile as she moved across to the room to deliver the ice water and menu.

Secretariat turned and watched her approach. Dark sunglasses reflected her silvery image and disguised his eyes. The glasses rested on a nose that could only kindly be described as aquiline. He removed the glasses and set them on the table.

Not until Elizabeth was at his table did she realize how big this man actually was. Massive shoulders fitted his height. The muscular biceps of his upper arms strained against a short-sleeved shirt stretched taut across a broad chest. Elizabeth imagined that someone of his build would have difficulty finding things that fit loosely. It was unfortunate that he couldn't afford to have his clothes custom-made.

"Good afternoon," she said as she handed him the menu and set the glass on the red-checkered tablecloth. Her heart lodged near her throat as his fingers innocently brushed hers. There was something indefinable about him that was almost intimidating. Not that he frightened her; intrigued was more the word.

"Hello." His smile revealed even, white teeth. He opened the menu and quickly scanned its contents. Without looking at her he said, "Don't worry, I don't bite."

"I didn't think you did," Elizabeth returned, resenting his attitude. She wasn't easily intimidated.

"I'll have coffee. Nothing more." A scowl made its way across his blunt face.

Elizabeth wrote down his order. He didn't look like the type to indulge in delicate French pastries.

As she returned to the counter, Elizabeth could feel his gaze leveled between her shoulder blades. She was accustomed to the admiring glances of men. She had what her grandmother referred to as the Wainwright coloring, a warm blend of colors that often generated curious stares. Her eyes were the palest blue and her hair a lush shade of golden brown, worn loose so that it curled in natural waves at her shoulders.

"Did you notice the muscles on him?" Elizabeth muttered under her breath to Gilly as she added a spoon to the side of the saucer. "I bet this guy wrestles crocodiles for a living."

Gilly pretended to be wiping down the long counter, her hand rubbing furiously as she stifled a giggle. "I think he's kinda cute."

"Yes, but you'd think boa constrictors were cuddly."

"He's different. Give me five minutes alone with him and I'd wager he's a real pussycat."

"Not me. He looks like he eats little girls like you for breakfast."

"You're teasing, aren't you?" Gilly's gaze flickered from the gleaming white counter in back of the pastry display.

Elizabeth didn't answer as she delivered the coffee. He drank it quietly, cupping the mug with his massive hands as he stared out the window. Standing, he left a handful of change on the table and turned to wink at Gilly.

"Good-bye." Gilly waved to him. "Come in again."

"I'd say you've got yourself an admirer," Elizabeth said, glancing from her friend to the retreating male figure.

"Not me," Gilly denied instantly. "He was watching you like a hawk. It's you who interests him, not me."

"Then I give Tarzan to you," Elizabeth spoke somberly. "Men like him are a bit much for me." She had heard about egotistical males with bodies like his. They spent hours every day building up their muscles so they could stand in front of a mirror and admire themselves.

Just before closing time, Gilly stuck her head around the kitchen door where Elizabeth was finishing emptying the condiments into the large containers.

"I bet he works on the docks."

"Who?"

"Don't be obtuse."

"Oh, Tarzan. I suppose," Elizabeth murmured, not overly interested. "I don't think he'll be back."

"He will," Gilly asserted confidently. "There was that look in his eyes. He's attracted to you, Beth. Even I noticed that." The implication was there that Elizabeth should have recognized it too.

Gilly was right. The next afternoon he arrived at the same time. Elizabeth was carrying a tray of dirty dishes to the counter when she brushed against his solid male figure.

"Excuse me." The low, almost gravelly tone left no doubt as to who was speaking.

"I'm the one at fault," Elizabeth muttered under her breath, disliking the uncomfortable warmth that emanated from where their bodies had touched. Easily six inches taller than she, Tarzan loomed above her. Most women would have been awed by his closeness. But the sensations she was feeling were more troubling than frightening. He wasn't wearing his dark glasses today. His guarded look as well as the color of his eyes were a surprise. Their amber shade resembled burnished gold. But the flecks that stared so intently at her were like those of a jungle beast. Again Elizabeth had the impression that this man could be dangerous. Gilly viewed him as a gentle giant, but Elizabeth wasn't nearly as confident.

"What did I tell you?" Gilly whispered with a know-it-all voice.

"I guess you know your ape-men," Elizabeth returned flippantly.

For a second Gilly looked stunned at Elizabeth's cynicism. "How can you look at someone as gorgeous as this guy and call him an ape?" Righteously, she tucked the menu under her arm. "I'm taking his order today," she announced, and she strolled across the floor.

Watching her friend's movements, Elizabeth had to stifle a small laugh. Gilly's walk couldn't be more obvious; she was interested in him, and before the afternoon was over Tarzan would know it.

"His name's Andrew Breed," Gilly cheerfully informed her as she scooted past Elizabeth. "But he says most everyone calls him Breed." She moved behind the counter before Elizabeth could respond.

Elizabeth was too busy with her own customers to notice much about either Gilly or Andrew Breed. Only once was she aware that he was studying her, his strong mouth quirked crookedly. His attention made her self-conscious. Once she thought he was going to ask her something, but if he was, the question went unasked. As he'd done the day before, he left the money for his coffee on the table and sauntered out of the café before Elizabeth was aware he'd gone.

The remainder of the afternoon dragged miserably. The weather was hot and humid, and Elizabeth could feel tiny beads of perspiration wet her upper lip. A long soak in the bath, a light meal, and television sounded more appealing by the minute. Elizabeth had spent most of her evenings looking for an apartment;

the more she learned about Gilly's plight living at home the more she wanted to help her young friend. Elizabeth hoped that if she found a place they could move in together and share the rent, but Gilly need never know the actual rent.

Elizabeth was quickly learning that Gilly hadn't underestimated the difficulty of finding a reasonably priced apartment in the city. She couldn't very well rent one for $1,500 a month and tell Gilly her share was $200. Her friend, although flighty, was smart enough to figure things out.

Gilly and Elizabeth worked together to close down the café for another night. Elizabeth's thoughts were preoccupied as Gilly chattered away excitedly about one thing or another. The girl's boundless enthusiasm affected everyone she met. Gilly was an amazing person.

In the dressing room in the back of the kitchen, Elizabeth sat, kicked off her shoes and rubbed her aching feet. Gilly hobbled around, one shoe on and the other off as she opened her purse and dug around looking for something in the bottom of the large bag.

"What's the big hurry?" Elizabeth inquired.

"What's the hurry?" Gilly stammered. "Breed'll be out front any minute. We're going to dinner."

"Breed?" Her heart did a tiny flip-flop. "You mean to say you're going out to dinner with someone you hardly know?"

"What do you think I was telling you?"

Elizabeth straightened and slipped her feet back into the new practical pumps she'd purchased with Gilly's approval. "I guess I wasn't paying any attention."

"I guess!" Gilly shook her head and did a quick glance in the small mirror. "Oh dear, I'll never make it on time." The petite oval face creased with concern. "Beth, do me a favor. Go out front and tell Breed I'm running a little late. I'll be there in a few minutes."

"Sure." Her response was clipped and short. Elizabeth didn't want to date Breed herself, but she wasn't sure how she felt about Gilly's seeing him. The thought was so ridiculous that she pinched her mouth closed, irritated with herself at her musings.

"You don't mind, do you?" Gilly jerked her head around to study Elizabeth.

"Of course not. It's the least I can do to smooth the course of true love."

"Not about that," Gilly said.

Elizabeth tipped her head to one side in confusion.

"I mean about me going out with Breed."

"Me mind?" Elizabeth asked, giving an indifferent shrug. "Why should I care one way or the other?"

Gilly arched both delicately designed brows. "Because it's really you he's interested in."

"You keep saying that," Elizabeth said, shaking her head in denial. "Either you've got some sixth sense or I'm completely dense."

Without hesitation, Gilly threw back her head, her tight curls bouncing. "You're dense."

Resolutely squaring her shoulders, Elizabeth headed for the front of the café. Evelyn followed her out to lock the door after her, just as Gilly stuck her head around the kitchen door. "He's coming," she cried. "I can see him across the street." Round, panic-stricken eyes pleaded with Elizabeth. "Keep him occupied, will you?"

"Don't worry." She called to Gilly and smiled at Evelyn on the other side of the glass door as he turned the lock. Evelyn looked at Elizabeth and playfully rolled his eyes.

When Elizabeth turned around, she was only a few inches from Breed. This man had the strangest effect on her. She wasn't sure how she felt about him. His appeal blossomed with every encounter. It hadn't taken her long to realize that her first impression of him as a muscle-bound egomaniac was completely wrong. Breed seemed almost unaware of the effect he had on women.

"Gilly will be ready in a minute. She's changing clothes now."

The tight corners of Breed's mouth edged upward. "No problem; I'm early."

Elizabeth folded her arms around her slim waist. "Gilly's looking forward to tonight." Realizing her telltale mannerisms, she quickly dropped her hands to her sides.

"I make you uncomfortable, don't I?"

Color rose from her neck, brightening her cheeks. "It's not that. I...I don't think I've ever known anyone quite like you."

"As big, you mean?"

"No, not that."

His strong, angular chin tilted downward fractionally. "And I don't think I've known anyone as beautiful as you." The words sounded low and soft.

Immediately Elizabeth sensed that he wished he could withdraw them. He hadn't intended to say that. She was sure of it.

"My size is intimidating," he stated flatly, taking a step in retreat. There was a strong suggestion of impatience in the way he moved. This was something she hadn't noted in the past. He was angry with himself.

Ignoring the strong, male profile, Elizabeth turned and looked into the cloudless blue sky.

"The weather..."

"How long..."

They both spoke at once.

"You first." Breed smiled, and a pleasant warmth invaded her limbs.

"I was going to say that I was enjoying the weather this summer. After all that talk about the California smog and San Francisco's famous fog, I wasn't sure what to expect."

"You're not from California?" He looked surprised.

Elizabeth didn't know why he should be; her light Boston accent wasn't difficult to decipher. "No, my roots are on the East Coast."

He nodded.

"Do you work on the wharf?" Conversation was easy with him; something else Elizabeth hadn't expected. "Gilly and I were trying to guess."

"I'm a longshoreman."

It was Elizabeth's turn to give a polite nod. "It must be hard work." What else would give him muscles like that?

Fresh as a dewy rosebud, Gilly floated out the door in a light-blue summer dress, her hair still wet from the shower. "Sorry to keep you waiting, Breed."

His amber eyes crinkled at the corners with a warm smile. "It was worth it," he said as he moved to her side, taking her hand in his.

Elizabeth wondered how Gilly could look so refreshed, then remembered there was a shower in the back of the kitchen.

Wiping a bead of perspiration from her forehead, Elizabeth gave Breed and Gilly a feeble smile. "Have fun, you two."

"Are you sure you won't join us?" Gilly said.

Elizabeth took a step backward. As crazy as it sounded, she was half tempted. "I can't tonight. I'm going to look at another apartment."

"Beth, it's hopeless," Gilly said, her voice emphatic.

Breed's eyes surveyed her with open interest. "Are you looking for an apartment?"

"Are we ever," Gilly proclaimed enthusiastically.

"Let me know what happens. I might be able to find something for you. My brother-in-law manages a building, and he told me he has a vacancy coming."

Gilly almost threw herself into his arms. "Really? Oh, Beth, what do you think?"

Elizabeth's smile wasn't nearly as enthusiastic. If Breed's in-law showed them the apartment, he was sure to mention the rent, and Elizabeth knew Gilly couldn't afford much.

"Let me check out this ad tonight, and we can talk about it later."

A half-hour later Elizabeth was soaking in a hot tub filled with a light-scented bubble bath. With the back of her head resting against the polished enamel bathtub, she closed her eyes, regretting that she hadn't gone with Breed and Gilly. She wouldn't turn down a second invitation.

Chapter Two

Oh, Beth!" Gilly exclaimed as she hurriedly stepped from room to room of the two-bedroom apartment in the marina district. "I can hardly believe how lucky you were to find this place. It's perfect."

Elizabeth was rather proud of it herself. The building was an older, brick structure that had recently been renovated. She'd been fortunate to find it, even more fortunate to have convinced Gilly and Gilly's parents that the rent was cheaper the first six months because there was still construction going on in the building. The simplicity of the apartment made her deception easier; Elizabeth could afford to pay three-quarters of the rent without Gilly ever being the wiser.

Polished wooden floors in the entryway led to a large carpeted living room that made liberal use of skylights.

"I still can't believe it," Gilly said as she slowly rotated, her head tilted back to view the boundless blue sky through the polished glass ceiling. "I never dreamed you'd find something like this. Did you see that kitchen?" She returned her attention to Elizabeth. "Even my mother doesn't have a microwave." With a deep sense of awe, she stepped into the kitchen and ran her hand along the spotless counter. "I can't believe how well everything is working out for us." Pausing to glance at her wristwatch, she shook her head. "I've got one last load to bring over. I shouldn't be more than an hour."

"Don't worry. I'll hold down the fort," Elizabeth returned absently.

There were several things she wanted to do herself, including grocery shopping. She could fill the cupboards and Gilly would have no way of knowing how much she'd spent. When they divided the total, Gilly wouldn't realize that she was only paying a fraction of the total. Elizabeth was enjoying the small duplicity. With a growing sense of excitement, she changed her clothes and started to make out an errand list. The Wainwrights were known for their contributions to charity, but this small deception with Gilly wasn't charity. She felt as though she owed Gilly something. If it hadn't been for Gilly, Elizabeth was convinced she would still be trapped in the sluggish indifference that had dominated her life these past months. Her mother would have liked Gilly. Elizabeth pulled herself up straight. She hadn't thought about her mother in weeks. The memory remained sharp, with the power to inflict deep emotional pain. Just then the doorbell chimed. Elizabeth couldn't imagine who it could be.

Her step quickened as she walked to the door and opened it.

"Hello, Breed." Her hand tightened on the glass doorknob.

He handed her a large bouquet of flowers. "Welcome to the neighborhood," he said with a boyish grin.

"You live around here?" Her voice caught softly in her throat as she accepted the flowers. "Come in, please. I'm not being much of a hostess." She stepped back to allow him to enter and closed the door with her foot. "Gilly isn't here, but you're welcome to come in and tour the place if you like."

A smile glinted from his eyes as he followed her into the kitchen. "I'd like."

Deftly, Elizabeth arranged the flowers and set them in the middle of the round kitchen table before leading the way through the apartment, glossing over the details.

"You're renting this for how much?"

Elizabeth's heart lodged near her stomach. Gilly had apparently said something to Breed about their rent. She gave a light, breezy laugh, or what she hoped sounded light and breezy, and repeated what she'd told Gilly.

"Funny, I didn't notice any construction." He stood at the picture window.

"Of course you didn't." Elizabeth continued the misconception while keeping her gaze lowered. "Even carpenters go home in the evening." She was rescued from any further explanation by Gilly, who breathlessly barged through the door carrying a large box.

"Let me help." Immediately Breed took it from her and helped her carry in the remaining boxes.

When they'd finished, Gilly strolled into the kitchen. "Breed offered to take us out to dinner. You'll come, won't you?"

Elizabeth's gaze flittered past Gilly to Breed. She was uncomfortably aware of the unspoken questions he was sending her way.

"Not this time."

Gilly exhaled a heavy breath and pushed the curls from the side of her face in an exasperated movement. "But you will soon, right?" She glanced from Breed to Elizabeth.

"Another time," Elizabeth agreed, pretending to make out a grocery list.

"Promise?" Gilly prompted.

"Promise," Elizabeth returned, unsure why she felt the way she did. There was something about Breed that troubled her. Not his size, although that in itself was intimidating. His eyes often held a mischievous glint, as if he knew something she didn't. Not that he was laughing at her—far from it. There was understanding, compassion, and sometimes she thought she caught a glimmer of something close to sympathy. Breed was a complicated man, and Elizabeth feared that if she investigated further she'd like him a lot more than she had a right to.

She should have realized that neither Gilly nor Breed would accept another refusal to join them. The following Saturday Gilly was adamant that Elizabeth join them for an outing to the beach.

"You're coming!" Gilly insisted, stuffing an extra beach towel in the bag.

"Gilly..." Elizabeth moaned.

"It's a gorgeous day. How can you even think about sitting at home when you can be lazing on the beach, soaking up the sun?"

"But I don't want to intrude."

"Intrude? Are you nuts? We want you to come."

Gilly had gone out with Breed twice in the last week. They'd wanted to include Elizabeth both times.

Elizabeth liked Breed. The intensity of her feelings both surprised and alarmed her. Each time Gilly and Breed went out they returned early enough to surprise Elizabeth. The three sat in the living room and talked while drinking coffee. At every meeting, Elizabeth grew more aware of him. Gilly had reacted naturally to the magnetic appeal of this man, but it had taken Elizabeth longer to recognize his potency.

Breed was a wonderful conversationalist. His experiences were broad and seemingly unlimited. Several times Elizabeth had to bite her tongue to keep from revealing more of herself and her background. In some ways she felt there wasn't anything she couldn't share with him.

Elizabeth didn't know what to make of Gilly's relationship with him. They seemed to enjoy one another's company and had formed an easy friendship. But Gilly was the world's friend. After Gilly and Breed had spent an evening together, Elizabeth would study her roommate closely. Gilly didn't appear to be falling in love, and Elizabeth found that conclusion comforting. Not that she was such an expert on love. There'd been several times she had wondered whether she was in love, but decided if she had to wonder that, she wasn't.

"Put on your swimsuit," Gilly shouted from the kitchen. "And hurry. Breed'll be here in ten minutes."

"You're suie you want me along?" Elizabeth continued to waver.

Gilly turned around and rolled her eyes theatrically. "Yes! You really do have a problem with the obvious, don't you?"

Elizabeth changed into her silky turquoise bikini. On the beaches of the Riviera the skimpy two-piece had been modest. Now, studying herself in the mirror, she felt naked and more than a little vulnerable.

Gilly gave a low wolf whistle. "Wow! That doesn't look like it came out of a Sears catalogue."

"There's not much to it." Elizabeth's gaze was questioning.

"I know. It's gorgeous—you're gorgeous."

"I'm not sure I should wear it...I've got a sun dress that would serve just as well."

"Elizabeth," Gilly cried. "Wear the bikini." She bit into a carrot stick. "Honestly, there are times I swear that you're the most insecure person I've ever met." She took the carrot stick out of her mouth and held it in her fingers like a cigarette. "By the way, where did you get that suit? I've never seen anything like it."

Elizabeth hesitated, her mind whirling in a thousand directions. "A little place...I don't remember the name."

"Well, wherever it is you shop sure has beautiful clothes."

"Thank you,' Elizabeth mumbled as she put on the white terrycloth cover-up. Quickly she changed the subject. "You're looking great yourself."

Gilly lowered her gaze to the rose-colored one-piece with a deep-veed neckline and halter top. "This old rag?"

"You just got that last week."

"I know, but next to you it might as well be a rag."

"Gilly, that's not true, and you know it."

"Yes, but look at you. You're perfect. I'd kill for a figure like that. There isn't anything I wouldn't sacrifice for long legs and a figure like yours."

Elizabeth was still laughing when Breed arrived. He paused and gave Gilly an appreciative glance. "I should have suggested the beach sooner. You look fantastic."

Gilly positively sparkled under his sensual appraisal. "Wait until you see Elizabeth's suit; she's the one with the glorious body."

Breed didn't comment, but exchanged a meaningful glance with Elizabeth that said more than words.

Admittedly, Elizabeth wanted to impress Breed. Deep within herself she yearned for his eyes to reveal the approval he had given Gilly. To divert her mind from its disconcerting course, she tied the sash to her cover-up and added the suntan lotion to the beach bag.

"I'm ready if you are," Elizabeth said to no one in particular. She continued to feel a little uneasy hedging in on Gilly's time with Breed. But she was pleased to be spending the day in the sun. In past summers she had prided herself on a luxurious tan. Already it was the third week of June, and she looked as pale as eggwhite.

An hour later they had spread a blanket on a crowded beach at Santa Cruz, sharing the sand with a thousand other sun-worshippers. Breed sat with his knees bent as Gilly smoothed lotion into his broad shoulders.

Mesmerized, Elizabeth couldn't tear her eyes away. Gilly's fingers blended the tanning oil with the thin sheen of perspiration that slicked his muscular back. She rubbed him with slow, firm strokes until Elizabeth's mouth went dry. The bronze skin rippled with the massaging movements, his flesh supple under Gilly's uncomplicated manipulations. Lean and hard, Breed was excitingly, sensuously, all male.

Elizabeth's breath caught in her throat as she felt Breed's gaze. His eyes roamed her face, pausing on the fullness of her lips. They were filled with silent messages meant only for her. They were messages Elizabeth couldn't decipher, afraid of their meaning. Her cheeks suffused with hot color and she dragged her eyes from his.

"You probably should put some lotion on, Elizabeth," Breed commented. The slight huskiness of his voice was the only evidence that he was as affected as she by their brief exchange.

"He's right," Gilly agreed. "When I've finished here, I'll do you."

Elizabeth was amused at the look of disappointment Breed cast her. He'd planned to do it himself, and Gilly had easily thwarted him.

After Gilly's quick application of lotion to her back, Elizabeth slathered her stomach and laid down. A forearm over her eyes blocked out the piercing rays of the afternoon sun. Pretending to be asleep, Elizabeth was only half listening as Breed and Gilly chatted about one thing or another.

"Hey, look," Gilly cried excitedly. "They've started a game of volleyball. You two want to play?"

"Not me," Elizabeth mumbled.

"You go ahead," Breed insisted.

A spray of sand hit Elizabeth's side as Gilly took off running. No doubt Gilly was as competent at sports as she was at everything else.

"Mind if I share the blanket with you?" Breed questioned softly.

"Of course not." Her mind was screaming for him to join Gilly at volleyball.

Breed stretched out beside her, so close their thighs touched. Elizabeth tensed, her long nails biting into her palms. Her nerves fired to life at the merest brush of his skin against hers. She attempted to scoot away, but granules of sand dug into her shoulder blade and she realized she couldn't go any farther on the blanket.

Never had she been more acutely aware of a man. Every sense was dominated by him. He smelled of spicy musk and fragrant tobacco. Did Breed smoke? Elizabeth couldn't remember seeing him smoke. Nothing had ever smelled more tantalizing.

Salty beads of perspiration wetted her upper lip, and she bit into the corner of her mouth. If he were to kiss her she would taste the salty flavor of his...Elizabeth sat up, unable to endure any more of these twisted games her mind was playing.

"I think I'll take a swim," she announced breathlessly.

"Running away?" Breed's gaze mocked her.

"Running?" she echoed innocently. "I thought I'd cool down."

"You're right. I could use a soak in cold water myself." With an agility she had difficulty understanding in a man his size, Breed pulled himself to his feet.

As Breed brushed the sand from the back of his legs, Elizabeth ran toward the ocean. With her long hair flying behind her, she laughed as she heard him shout for her to wait. The water was only a matter of a few feet away, and they hit the pounding surf together.

The spray of cool water that splashed against her thighs took Elizabeth's breath, and she stopped abruptly. Certainly the ocean waters off the California coast were supposed to be warmer than this.

Breed dived into an oncoming wave and surfaced several feet away. He turned and waited for her to join him.

Following his lead, she swam to him, keeping her head above water as her smooth, even strokes cut into the swelling ocean.

"What's the matter?" he called. "Afraid to get your hair wet?"

"I want to resemble Esther Williams, not Boy George."

He laughed, and Elizabeth couldn't remember hearing a more pleasant sound.

"You should laugh more often."

"Me?" A frown darkened his eyes. "You're the one who needs a few lessons on having fun." He swam to her and placed a hand around her waist. "Let's take this wave together."

Given no option, Elizabeth was thrust into the oncoming wall of water. As they went under the giant surge, she panicked, frantically lashing out with her arms and legs.

Breed pulled her to the surface. "Are you all right?"

"No," she screamed, coughing and choking on her words. Saltwater stung her eyes. Her hair fell in wet tendrils over her face. "You did that on purpose," she accused him angrily.

"Of course I did," he countered. "It's supposed to be fun."

"Fun!" she spat. "Marie Antoinette's walk to the guillotine was more fun than that."

Breed sobered. "Come on. I'll take you back to the blanket."

"I don't want to go back." Another wave hit her, and her body rolled with it, her face going below the surface just as it crested. Again she came up coughing.

Breed joined her and gripped her waist. "This is too much for you."

"It isn't," she sputtered. "If this is supposed to be fun, then I'll do it." With both hands she pushed the wet, stringy hair from her face. The feel of his body touching hers was doing crazy things to her equilibrium. The whole world began to sway. It might have been the effect of the ocean, but Elizabeth doubted it.

"Will you teach me, Breed?" she requested with a husky whisper. She felt his body tense as the movement of the Pacific tide brought him close.

"Hold on," he cried as another wave engulfed them.

Elizabeth slipped her arms around his neck and held her breath. Breed's hands surrounded her protectively, pressing her into the shelter of his arms. Their feet kicked in unison and they broke the surface together.

"How was that?" he asked.

Her eyes still closed, Elizabeth nodded. "Better." Why was she kidding herself? This was heaven. Being held by Breed was the most perfect experience she could remember. That took her by surprise. She'd been held more intimately by others.

Slowly she opened her eyes. Breed pushed the hair from her face. "You're slippery," he murmured, pulling her tighter into his embrace. His massive hands found their place at the small of her back.

"So are you. It must be the suntan lotion." Her breasts brushed his torso and shivers of tingling desire raced through her. Such complete physical response was as pleasant as it was unexpected.

"Watch out," Breed called as they took the next wave. With their bodies intertwined, they rode the swell together.

A crooked smile was slanting Breed's mouth as they surfaced. Again his fingers freed her face from the long strands of wet hair. He tucked them behind her ear, also removing the wet strands from her shoulder and exposing her neck.

Elizabeth could feel the pulse near her throat flutter wildly. Breed pressed his fingertips to it and raised his eyes to her. In their golden depths she read several things: desire, regret, surprise. He seemed to be as unprepared for this physical attraction as she.

His mouth gently explored the pounding pulse in her neck. Moaning softly, Elizabeth rolled her head to one side. His lips teased her skin, shooting unanticipated shivers of delight over her. When he stopped, his eyes again sought hers.

"You taste salty."

Responding words refused to form, and it was all she could do to nod.

Breed had come with Gilly. Elizabeth had no right to be in the ocean with him, wanting him to kiss her so badly she could feel it in every pore of her body.

"We should go back." She heard the husky throb in her voice.

"Yes," he agreed.

But they didn't move.

Breed's crooked grin returned. "Did you have fun?"

Elizabeth nodded.

"I'm sorry about your hair."

"Are you trying to tell me I no longer resemble Esther Williams?"

"No, but if you want the truth, I've never seen you look more beautiful."

Elizabeth's skin chilled, then flushed with warmth. Breed's words had the power to regulate even her body temperature.

"I think you're being overly kind," Elizabeth murmured, realizing her voice contained a soft catch that revealed the effect of his words.

They lingered in the water as if each wanted to delay as long as possible the return to reality. Then together they walked out of the surf, hand in hand.

When Breed reached their blanket, he retrieved the towels. "Here." He handed her a thick one and buried his face in his own.

Sitting on the blanket, Elizabeth dug through the beach bag and came up with a comb. She was running it through the length of her hair when Gilly came rushing up. A tall, blond male was beside her.

"Breed and Elizabeth, this is Peter."

"Hi, Peter." Breed rose to his feet, standing several inches taller than the suntanned blond. The two men shook hands. For a second Breed looked from Gilly to Peter, then back again. His brows pulled into a thick frown.

"Peter invited me to join him," Gilly explained enthusiastically. "He said he'd take me home later. You two don't mind, do you?"

Elizabeth's eyes widened with shock. Did Gilly honestly believe she should come to the beach with one man and leave with another?

"We don't mind," Breed answered for them both.

"You're sure?" Gilly seemed to want Elizabeth's approval.

"Go ahead," Elizabeth murmured, but her eyes refused to meet Gilly's.

"You guys looked like you were having fun in the water."

A gust of wind whipped Elizabeth's wet hair across her face. She pushed it aside. The action gave her vital moments to compose herself. Obviously Gilly had been watching her in the ocean with Breed. Worse, it could be the reason her roommate had decided to go with Peter. She couldn't allow that to happen.

"We had a wonderful time." Again Breed answered for them both.

"I'll see you tonight, then," Gilly said, walking backward as she spoke.

Frustrated, Elizabeth called out for Gilly to wait, but the girl ignored her, turned, and took off running. "We can't let her do that," she shouted at Breed.

"What?" A speculating light entered his eyes.

"What's the matter with the both of you? Gilly's going off with a complete stranger. It isn't safe." She tugged the comb through her hair angrily. "Heaven knows what she's walking into. You didn't have to be so willing to agree to her crazy schemes. I'm not going to leave this beach without her."

"She's twenty and old enough to take care of herself." His low voice contained a note of vague concern.

"She's too damn trusting."

Ignoring her, Breed brought out the bucket of chicken he'd brought. "Want a piece?" he questioned, biting on a chicken leg.

"Breed." Elizabeth was quickly losing her patience. They were an hour from San Francisco, and he was literally handing Gilly over to a stranger.

"All right." He expelled his breath forcefully and closed the lid on the food. "Gilly knows Peter. I introduced them last week."

"What?" Elizabeth gasped. None of this was making sense.

"The last time I went out with Gilly, we were really meeting Peter."

"I don't believe this."

"I didn't exactly need an expert to see that it was going to take weeks of coming to the Patisserie and eating those flaky croissants before you'd agree to go out with me."

"What's that got to do with anything?"

"Plenty." Breed didn't sound thrilled to be revealing his actions. "I don't blame you. I am big and a little terrifying at first."

Elizabeth wanted to explain that it wasn't his size that intimidated her, but she didn't know how to account for her reticence. She couldn't very well explain that it was his eyes in a certain light. "So you dated Gilly instead?"

He nodded. "She knew that first night it was you I was interested in. We planned this today." The tone of his voice relayed his unwillingness to play the game.

No wonder Gilly had been so anxious for her to join them on every outing she'd taken with Breed.

"But you looked surprised when Gilly brought Peter over." Elizabeth recalled the partially concealed question his eyes shot at Gilly and Peter.

"Those two should be nominated for Academy Awards. They were supposed to have been long-lost friends." His jaw tightened as he turned away from her to look out over the ocean. His profile was strong and masculine.

"You needn't have told me." His honesty was a measure of how much he did care.

"No, I didn't. But I felt you had the right to know." His arms circled his bent knees. "I hope Gilly realizes what a good friend you are."

Lightly, Elizabeth's fingers traced the corded muscles of Breed's back. A smile danced at the edges of her mouth. "No, I think you've got the facts wrong. It's me who needs to thank Gilly."

He turned just enough so that he could view her lying on the blanket, looking up at him.

"How could I have been so stupid?" She whispered the question, staring into the powerful face of this gentle giant.

He lay on his stomach beside her.

"Have you always been big?"

"Have you always had freckles on your nose?" He aptly turned tables on her. His index finger brushed the tip of her nose.

Elizabeth's hand flew to her face. "They're terrible. I've hated them all my life."

"And disguise them rather well."

"Of course I do. What woman wants orange dots glowing from her nose?"

"They're beautiful."

"Breed," she said, raising herself up so that she rested her weight on her elbows. "How can you say something like that?"

"Maybe it's because I find you to be surprisingly delightful. You're refreshingly honest, hard-working, and breathtakingly beautiful."

Elizabeth recalled all the flattery she'd been given in her life by men who had something to gain by paying her attention. A large inheritance was coming to her someday. That was enough incentive to make her overwhelmingly attractive to any man.

But here she was on a crowded California beach with someone who didn't know her from Eve. And he sincerely found her beautiful. She cast her gaze downward, suddenly finding her deception distasteful. A lone tear found its way to the corner of her eye.

"Elizabeth, what's wrong?"

She didn't know how she could explain. "Nothing," she returned softly. "The wind must have blown a particle of sand in my eye." By tilting her chin upward toward the brilliant blue sky, she was able to quell any further emotion.

Resuming her sun-soaking position, Elizabeth lay on her back. Breed rolled over, positioning himself so close she felt his skin brush hers.

"Comfortable?" he asked.

"Yes."

Breed's large hand reached for hers so that they lay, fingers entwined. Neither spoke, but the communication between them was stronger than words.

Elizabeth must have dozed.

"Elizabeth." A hand at her shoulder shook her lightly. "If you don't put something on, you'll get burned."

Struggling to a sitting position, she discovered Breed kneeling above her, holding out her terrycloth cover-up. "You better wear this."

She placed it over her head. "Is there any of that chicken left?"

"Are you hungry?"

"Starved. I was in such a rush this morning, I didn't eat breakfast."

Opening the cooler, Breed fixed her a plate of food that was enough to feed her for three meals.

Elizabeth didn't voice her qualms as she took a bite of the chicken. It was fabulous. But she couldn't decide if it was the meal or the man.

The sun had sunk into a pink sky when Breed pulled up to the curb of her apartment.

"You'll come in for coffee, won't you?" Elizabeth issued the invitation, but they both knew that he wasn't coming inside for coffee.

She continued with the pretense, filling the kettle with water and placing it on the stove. She turned to discover his smoldering amber eyes burning over her. Her heart skipped a beat, then accelerated wildly at the promise she read there.

Wordlessly, she walked into his arms. This was the first time he'd held her outside the water, and she was amazed at how perfectly their bodies fitted together. The top of her head was tucked neatly under his chin.

Her smile was provocative as she slipped her arms around his neck and tilted her head back to look up at him.

His eyes were smiling back at her.

"What's so amusing?"

"The glow from your freckles is blinding me."

"If I wasn't so eager for you to kiss me, I'd make you pay for that remark."

Breed lowered his mouth to an inch above hers. "I have a feeling I'm going to pay anyway," he murmured as he tightly wrapped his arms around her.

Being so close to this vibrant male was enough to disturb her senses. She tried to ignore the myriad of sensations his touch was producing. As silly and crazy as it seemed, she felt like Sleeping Beauty waiting for the kiss to awaken her after a hundred years.

Tenderly his mouth brushed over her eyelid, causing her lashes to flutter shut. Next he kissed her nose. "I love those freckles," he whispered.

Lastly he kissed her mouth with a masterful possession that was everything she had dreamed a kiss could be. It was a kiss worth waiting a hundred years for. He was gentle, yet possessive. Pliant, yet hard. Responsive, yet restrained.

"Oh, Breed," she whispered achingly.

"I know." He breathed against her temple. "I wasn't expecting this either."

Elizabeth closed her eyes and took in the mingled scent of spicy musk and saltwater. With her head pressed close to his heart, she could hear the uneven beat and knew he was as overwhelmed as she at how right everything was between them.

"I should go," he mumbled into her hair. He didn't need to add that he meant he should leave while he still had the power to pull himself out of her arms.

"Can I see you tomorrow?"

Eagerly Elizabeth nodded.

He pulled away. "Walk me to the door."

She did as he requested. He kissed her again, but not with the intensity of the first time. Then, lightly, he ran one finger over her cheek. "Tomorrow," he whispered.

"Tomorrow," she repeated, closing the door after him.

Chapter Three

Elizabeth adjusted the strap of her pink linen summer dress as Gilly strolled down the hall and leaned against the doorjamb, studying her. "Hey, you look fantastic."

"Thanks." Elizabeth's smile was uneasy. Breed had been on her mind all day, dominating her thoughts, filling her consciousness. Yesterday at the beach may have been a fluke, the result of too much sun and the attention of an attractive male. Yet Elizabeth couldn't remember a day she had enjoyed more. Certainly not in the last two years. Breed made her feel alive again. This morning she'd been cooking her breakfast and humming. She couldn't remember the last time she'd felt so content. When she was with Breed she wanted to laugh and throw caution to the wind.

Continuing to date him was doing exactly that. Elizabeth couldn't see herself staying in San Francisco past the summer. When it came time to return to Boston, her heart could be so entangled with Breed that leaving would be intolerable. No, Elizabeth decided, she had to protect herself...and Breed. He didn't know who she was and she could end up hurting him. She couldn't allow herself to fall in love with him. Whatever potential there was to this relationship had to be guarded. She couldn't allow this attraction to develop into anything more than a light flirtation.

"I sure wish I knew where you got your clothes," Gilly continued to chatter. "They're fantastic."

Elizabeth ignored the comment. "Do you think I'll need the jacket?" The matching pink top was casually draped over her index finger as Elizabeth's gaze sought Gilly's.

Gilly gave a careless shrug, crossing her arms and legs as she gave Elizabeth a thorough inspection. "I think I'd probably take it. You can never be certain what the weather's going to do. Besides, Breed may keep you out to the early-morning hours."

"Not when I have to work tomorrow, he won't," Elizabeth returned confidently.

The doorbell chimed just as Elizabeth finished rolling the lip gloss across the fullness of her bottom lip.

"I'll get it," Gilly called from the kitchen.

Placing her hands against the side of the dresser, Elizabeth inhaled, deeply and soothingly, and commanded her pounding heart to be still. The way she reacted to Breed, someone would think she was a sixteen-year-old who had just been asked out by the captain of the football team.

"It's Breed." Gilly sauntered into Elizabeth's room.

Elizabeth gave herself one final inspection in the dresser mirror. "I thought it must be." Folding her jacket over her forearm, she walked into the living room, where Breed was waiting.

"Hi," she said as casually as possible. Damn, he looked good. The earthy sensuality about him was more evident now than the dreams her mind had conjured up the previous night. Suddenly Elizabeth felt tongue-tied and frightened. She could so easily come to love this giant of a man.

"Beth didn't say where the two of you were going," Gilly said before biting into a crisp apple.

"I thought we'd take in the outdoor concert at the Sigmund Stern Grove. A cabaret sextet I'm familiar with is scheduled for today. That is"—he hesitated and caught Elizabeth's eye—"unless you have any objection."

"That sounds great." By some miracle Elizabeth found her voice. The corded muscles of Breed's massive shoulders relaxed. If Elizabeth didn't know better she would have guessed that he was as nervous about this meeting as she. Breed rotated his wrist to glance at his watch. "If we plan to get a seat in the stands then I suggest we leave now."

Gilly followed them to the door. "I won't wait up for you," she whispered, just loud enough for Elizabeth to hear.

"I won't be late," Elizabeth countered with a saccharine-sweet smile, discounting Gilly's assumption that she wouldn't be home until the wee hours of the morning.

Breed opened the door to a late-model, mud-splattered, army-green Jeep and glanced up at her quizzically. "I had to bring Hilda today. Do you mind?"

A Jeep! The urge to laugh was so strong she had to hold in her breath. She'd never ridden in one in her life. "Sure, it looks like fun."

Breed's hand supported the underside of her elbow as she climbed inside the vehicle. A vague disturbance fluttered along her nerve-endings at his touch, although impersonal. A covering had been placed on the seat to protect her dress. His thoughtfulness touched her heart. The problem was, almost everything about this man touched her heart.

Once she was seated inside the open Jeep, Elizabeth's eyes were level with Breed's. She turned and smiled as some of the nervous tension flowed from her.

When the warm possession of his mouth claimed her lips, Elizabeth's senses were overwhelmed with a rush of pleasure. The kiss, although brief, was ardent and left her weak and shaking. Abruptly, Breed stepped back, as though his actions had surprised him as much as they did her.

Dazed, she blinked her rounded eyes at him. "What was that for?" she asked breathlessly.

Breed walked around to the other side of the Jeep and climbed inside without effort. His hands gripped the steering wheel as he turned and grinned at her. "For being such a good sport. To be honest, I thought you'd object to Hilda."

"To a fine lady like Hilda?" Elizabeth teased. A trace of color returned to her bloodless cheeks. "Never. Why do you call her Hilda?"

"I don't know." He lifted one shoulder in a half-shrug. "Her temperament's a lot like a woman's. It seems when I least expect trouble is when she decides to break down." The mocking glint of laughter touched his amber eyes. "She's as temperamental as they come."

"Proud, too," Elizabeth commented, but her words were drowned out by the roar of the engine. Hilda coughed, sputtered, and then came to life with a vengeance.

"See what I mean?" Breed muttered disparagingly as he shifted gears and pulled onto the street.

By the time they'd reached the park, Elizabeth's carefully styled hair was in terrible disarray. The wind had whipped it from the loose chignon and carelessly tossed it about her neck and face.

"You all right?" Breed asked with a mischievous look in his eye.

Elizabeth opened the clasp to her purse and took out a brush. "Just give me a minute to comb my hair and scrape the bugs from my teeth and I'll be fine."

The pleasant sound of his laughter caused the sensitive muscles of her flat stomach to tighten. "I think Hilda must like you," he said as he climbed out and slammed the door. "I know I do." The words were issued under his breath, as if he didn't mean for Elizabeth to hear them.

The park was crowded, the free concerts obviously a popular program of the Parks and Recreation Department. Already the stands were filled, and it didn't look as if Elizabeth and Breed would find seating together. Other couples had spread blankets on the lush green grass.

A guiding hand at her elbow led Elizabeth toward the stands. "I think we might find a seat for you over here."

"Breed." She stopped him and turned slightly. "Couldn't we take the blanket from Hilda and sit on the lawn?"

"You'd want to do that?" He looked shocked.

"Why not?"

His eyes surveyed her dress, lingering momentarily on the jutting swell of her breasts. "But you might ruin your dress."

A flush of heat warmed her face at the bold look he was giving her. "Let me worry about that," she murmured, her voice only slightly affected.

"If you're sure." His eyes sought hers.

"Get the blanket, and I'll find us a place to sit."

They settled onto the grass and waited silently for the music to start. Elizabeth had sat in the great musical halls of Europe and throughout the United States, but rarely had she anticipated a concert more. When the first melodious strains of a violin echoed through the park, she straightened and closed her eyes.

The sextet proved to be as versatile as they were talented. The opening selection was a selection of classical numbers that Elizabeth recognized and loved. Enthusiastic applause showed the audience's approval. Then the leader came to the front and introduced the next numbers, a selection of musical scores from popular movies.

Elizabeth shifted her position, the hard ground causing her to fold her legs one way and then another.

"Here," Breed whispered, situating himself so that he was directly behind her, his legs to one side. "Use me for support." His hands ran down her bare arms as he eased her body weight against his. After a while she didn't know which score was louder, the one the musicians were playing or the one in her heart.

After the hour-long concert, Breed took her to a restaurant that he claimed served the best Mexican food this side of the Rio Grande.

"What did you think?" he asked as they sat across from one another in the open-air restaurant, eating cheese enchiladas and refried beans.

A gentle breeze ruffled Elizabeth's sandy hair about her shoulders as she set her fork aside. "How do I feel about the concert or the food?"

"The concert." Breed pushed his plate aside, already finished. Elizabeth was only half done.

"It was great. The whole afternoon's been wonderful." Her hands cupped a tall glass of iced tea. Breed would be taking her home soon, and already she was dreading it. This day had been more enjoyable than all of the last six months, and she didn't want it to end. Every minute they were together was better than the one before. It sounded silly and maudlin, but Elizabeth didn't know how else to describe her feelings. Deliberately she took a long sip of her drink and set her fork aside.

"Are you finished already?"

Elizabeth's gaze skimmed her half-full plate, and she nodded, her appetite gone.

"I suppose we should think about getting you back to the apartment."

Elizabeth's heart sang at the reluctance in his voice. For one stimulating moment their gazes met and locked. She didn't want to go home and he didn't want to take her.

"How about a walk along the beach?" he suggested with only a hint of reluctance.

Elizabeth demonstrated no such hesitation. Sometimes the look in his eye made her wonder if he wanted to be with her or not. "Yes, I'd like that."

Hilda delivered them safely to an ocean beach about fifteen minutes outside the city. Others apparently had the same idea; several couples were strolling the sandy beach, their arms wrapped around one another's waists.

"Do you need to scrape the bugs from your teeth this time?" Breed asked as he shifted gears and turned off the engine. A smile was lurking at the edges of his sensuous mouth.

"No," she replied softly, "I've discovered that the secret of riding in Hilda is simply to keep my mouth closed."

Breed's responding smile only served to remind her of the strength and raw virility that were so much a part of him. Her gaze rested admiringly on the smoothly hewn angles of his face as he climbed out of the Jeep and came around to her side. She must have been crazy to have ever thought of him as an ape-man. The thought produced a grimace of anger at herself.

"Is something wrong?" Breed seemed sensitive to even her thoughts.

"It's nothing," she said, dismissing the question, not meeting his gaze.

Again his touch was impersonal as he guided her down a semi-steep embankment. A small creek of swiftly flowing water separated them from the main part of the beach.

Elizabeth hesitated as she searched for the best place to cross.

"What's the matter?" Breed teased with a vaguely challenging lilt to his voice. "Are you afraid of getting your feet wet?"

"Of course not," she denied instantly. "Well, maybe a little," she amended with a sheepish smile. It wasn't the water as much as the uncertainty of how deep and swift it ran.

"Allow me," Breed said as he swept her into his arms. One arm supported her back and the other her knees. Her hands flew automatically to his neck.

"Breed," she hissed under her breath. "What are you doing?"

"What any gallant gentleman would do for a lady in distress. I'm escorting you to safety." His amber eyes were dancing with mischief. He took a few steps and teetered, causing Elizabeth to grip his neck harder.

"Breed," she cried. "I'm too heavy. Put me down."

His chiseled mouth quirked in a teasing movement as he took a few more hurried steps and delivered her safely to the other side. When he set her down, Elizabeth noticed that his shoes were soaking wet.

"You *are* a gallant knight, aren't you?" The inflection of her voice made the question a statement of fact.

Something so brief that Elizabeth thought she'd imagined it flickered in his expression. It came and went so quickly she couldn't decipher its meaning, if there was one.

The dry sand dug deep into her sandals, and after only a few steps Elizabeth paused to take them off. Breed did the same, removing his shoes and socks and setting them beside a large rock. Elizabeth carelessly tossed hers with his, unconcerned.

They didn't say anything for a long time as they strolled, their hands linked. Breed positioned himself so that he took the brunt of the strong breeze that came off the water.

Elizabeth had no idea how far they'd gone. The sky was a glorious shade of pink. The blinding rays of the sinking sun cast its golden shine over them as they continued to stroll. The sight of the lowering sun produced a breathless sigh of wonder from Elizabeth as they paused to watch it sink beyond the horizon.

Watching the sun set had seemed like such a little thing, and not until this moment, with this man at her side, had Elizabeth realized how gloriously wondrous it was.

"Would you like to rest for a while before we head back?" Breed suggested. She agreed with a nod, and he cleared her a space in the dry sand.

With her arms cradling her knees, Elizabeth looked into a sky that wasn't yet dark. "How long will it be before the stars come out?"

"Not long," Breed answered in a low whisper, as if he were afraid words would diminish the wonder of the evening. Leaning back, he rested his weight on the palms of his hands as he looked toward the pounding waves of the ocean. "What made you decide to come to San Francisco?" he asked unexpectedly.

Elizabeth felt her long hair dance against the back of her neck in the breeze. "My mother. She spent time here the summer before she married my father, and loved it." Her sideward glance encountered deep, questioning eyes. "Is something wrong?"

Breed was still. "Are you planning on getting married?"

Elizabeth wasn't sure she was comfortable with this line of questioning. "Yes," she answered honestly.

Breed sat up, and Elizabeth noticed that his mouth had twisted wryly. "I wish to hell you'd said something before now." The steel edge of his voice couldn't be disguised.

"Well, doesn't everyone?"

"Everyone what?" The fragile control of his patience was stretched taut.

Scooting closer to his side, Elizabeth pressed her head against his shoulder. "Doesn't everyone think about getting married at one time or another?"

"What's this got to do with Mr. Boston Baked Bean sitting at home waiting for you?"

"Mr. Boston Baked Bean?" Elizabeth broke into delighted peals of laughter. "Honestly, Breed, I was teasing. There's no one."

"You little brat," Breed groaned as he turned and pressed her back against the sand. Her startled cry of protest was smothered by his plundering mouth. Immediately Elizabeth's arms circled his neck as his lips rocked over hers in an exchange of kisses that stirred her to the core of her soul.

Restlessly his hands roamed her spine as he half lifted her from the soft cushion of the sandy beach. Elizabeth arched against him as he sensually chewed on her lower lip, teasing her with biting kisses that promised but didn't relieve the building need she had for him.

"Breed," she moaned as her hands cupped his face, directing his hungry mouth to hers. Anything to satisfy this ache within her. A deep groan slipped from his throat as Elizabeth outlined his lips with the tip of her tongue.

Breed tightened his hold, and his mouth feasted hungrily on hers. He couldn't seem to give enough or take enough as he relaxed his grip and pressed her into the sand. One hand sought and found her breast, which swelled eagerly at his touch. Desire, raw and intense, ran through her bloodstream, spreading a demanding fire as he explored the sensitive cord of her neck and paused at the scented hollow of her throat.

Elizabeth's nails dug into his back as she shuddered with uninhibited longing.

The roughness of his calloused hand brushed the hair from her face. "I shouldn't have done that," he whispered. His voice was filled with regret. With a heavy sigh, he eased his weight from her. "Did I hurt you?" He helped her into a sitting position, but his hand remained on the curve of her shoulder as if he couldn't let go.

"You wouldn't hurt me," she answered in a voice so weak she paused and repeated herself. "I'm not hurt." Lovingly her finger traced the tight line of his jaw. "What's wrong? You look like you're sorry."

He nestled her into his embrace, holding her as he had at the concert, his arms wrapped around her from behind. His chin brushed rhythmically against the crown of her head.

"Are you sorry?" she repeated the question.

"No," he answered her in a disturbed whisper after a long time, and Elizabeth wondered if he was telling the truth.

Without either of them aware of it, darkness had descended around them. "The stars are out," Elizabeth commented, disliking the finely strung tension the silence produced. "When I was younger I used to lean out my bedroom window and try to count the stars."

"I suppose that was a good excuse to stay out late," Breed said thickly, continuing to rub his chin against her hair.

Elizabeth smiled to herself but didn't comment.

His embrace slackened. "Do you want to go?"

"No." Her response was immediate. "Not yet," she added, her voice losing some of its intensity. She shifted her position so that she lay back, her head supported by his lap as she gazed into the brilliant heavens. "It really is a gorgeous night."

"Gorgeous," Breed repeated, but she noted he was looking down on her when he spoke. "You certainly have a way of going to my head, woman."

"Do I?" She sprang to a sitting position. "Oh, Breed, do I really?"

He took her hand and placed it over his pounding heart. "That should answer you."

She let her hands slide over his chest and around his neck. Twisting, she turned and playfully kissed him.

"But the question remains if I do the same thing to you." Breed asked, his voice only slightly husky.

Elizabeth paused and shifted to a kneeling position at his side. Their eyes met in the gilded glow of the moon. "What does this tell you?" she said, more serious than she had been in her life. Taking his hand, she pressed it against the underside of her breast, holding it there as he cupped it and inhaled a quivering breath.

"It tells me"—he hesitated as if gathering his resolve—"that it's time to go," Breed said, bouncing to his feet, then offering her a hand to help her up.

With a smile, Elizabeth fitted her fingers into his.

The walk back seemed to take forever. Surely they hadn't gone this far.

"Isn't that Hilda?" she asked, pointing to the highway up ahead.

"Couldn't be." Breed's eyes squinted against the dark. "We haven't gone far enough yet."

"Far enough," she repeated incredulously. "We couldn't possibly have wandered much farther than this." Their portion of the beach was deserted now, although Elizabeth noted a few small fires in the distance, affirming that there were others around. "Isn't that the rock where we left our shoes?" She pointed at the large boulder directly ahead of them.

"No." Breed was adamant. "We've at least another half mile to go."

Another half mile, Elizabeth's mind shouted. Already a chill had rushed over her bare arms, and the sand squishing between her toes was decidedly wet. The surf was coming in, driving them farther and farther up the beach.

"I'm sure you're wrong," she told him with more confidence than she was feeling. "That's got to be the rock." She was unable to chase the slight quiver from her voice.

Angrily, Breed stripped his shirt from his arms and placed it around her bare shoulders. "You're freezing." He made it sound like an accusation. "For heaven's sake, why didn't you say something?"

"Because I knew you'd do something silly like rip off your shirt and give it to me," she shot back testily. "That's the rock, I'm sure of it," she reiterated, hurrying ahead. The only light available was from the crescent-shaped moon, and when she knelt down and discovered a sock she leapt triumphantly to her feet. "Ah, ha!" She dangled it in front of his nose. "What did I tell you!"

"That's not mine," Breed returned impatiently. "Good grief, Elizabeth, look at the size. That belongs to a child. That thing wouldn't fit my foot."

"This is the rock," she stated adamantly. "It's got to be."

"Fine." Breed's voice was decidedly chilly. "If this is the rock, then our shoes would be here. Right?" He crossed his arms and glared at her with marked tolerance.

Boldly, Elizabeth met his glare. "Someone could have taken them," she stated evenly, feeling suddenly righteous and the more unemotional of the two.

"Elizabeth." He paused and inhaled a calming breath. "Trust me. The rock and Hilda are about a half-mile up the beach. If you'll quit arguing with me and walk a little way you'll see that I know what I'm doing."

"No." Elizabeth knotted her fists at her side in angry resolve. "I'm tired and I'm cold and I think you've entirely lost your sense of direction. If you feel this isn't the rock, then go ahead and go. I'll be waiting for you here."

"You're not staying alone."

"I'm not going with you."

His eyes became hard points of steel, then softened. "Come on, it's only a little ways."

"No." She stamped her foot and splashed grit and sand against her bare leg from an incoming wave.

"You're not staying."

"Breed, listen to reason," she pleaded.

A wave crashed against his leg and he shook his head grimly.

"All right," Elizabeth conceded graciously. "Let's make a wager. Are you game?"

"Why shouldn't I be? You're wrong." The mood lightened immediately. "What do you want to bet?"

"I'll march the unnecessary half-mile up the beach with you. But on the offchance you're wrong, you must agree to carry me piggyback on the return trip. Agreed?"

"Just a minute here." A smile twitched at the corners of his mouth. "What do I get if I'm right?"

"A personal apology?" she suggested, confident she wouldn't need to make one.

His look was thoughtful. "Not good enough."

Elizabeth slowly moistened her lips and gently swayed her hips. "Ten slow kisses in the moonlight."

Breed shook his head. "That's too good."

Elizabeth laughed. "Are you always so hard to please?"

"No," he grumbled. "Come on, we can argue as we walk." He draped his arm over her shoulders, pulling her close. Elizabeth wasn't sure if it was because he was as cold as she or if he simply wanted her near his side. She tucked her arm around his waist, enjoying the cool feel of his skin against her.

"It's a good thing you've got those freckles," he said seriously about five minutes later. "Without those lighting the way, we'd be lost for sure."

In spite of herself, Elizabeth laughed. Breed had the ability to do that to her. If someone else had made a similar comment she would have been angry and hurt. But not Breed.

Ten minutes later they spied another large boulder in the distance.

"What did I tell you?" Breed oozed confidence.

"Don't be so sure of yourself," Elizabeth returned, only slightly unnerved.

"If my eyes serve me right, someone was kind enough to place our shoes on top so that they wouldn't be swept out with the tide."

Elizabeth's confidence cracked.

"Listen, Sacajawea. If you ever get lost, promise me you'll stay in one place."

"I get the message," she grumbled.

"Promise me," he said more forcefully. "I swear you'd argue with Saint Peter."

"Well, you're no saint," she shot back.

His grip tightened as his eyes looked into hers. "Don't remind me," he murmured just before claiming her lips in a hungry kiss that left her weak and breathless. "You owe me nine," he mumbled against her hair.

By the time they made it up to the highway and Hilda, found an all-night restaurant, and had coffee, it was well after one. And it was close to two when Elizabeth peeled back the covers to her bed.

When the alarm went off a few hours later, Elizabeth was sure the time was wrong. Her eyes burned and she felt as if she'd hardly slept.

Gilly was up and dressed by the time Elizabeth staggered into the kitchen and poured herself a cup of strong coffee.

"What time did you get in?" she asked cheerfully.

"Two," Elizabeth mumbled almost inaudibly.

"I thought you were the one who insisted on an early night," Gilly said in a teasing know-it-all voice.

"Do you have to be so happy in the morning?" Elizabeth grumbled, taking her first sip of coffee, nearly scalding her lip.

"When are you seeing Breed again?"

He hadn't said anything the night before about another date. But they would be seeing one another again; Elizabeth had never been more sure of anything. A smile flitted across her face at the memory of their heated discussion about the rock. She could feel Gilly's gaze skimming over her.

"Obviously you're seeing him soon," Gilly announced, heading toward her bedroom.

Breed came into the café later that afternoon at the time he usually arrived.

He gave Elizabeth a warm smile and yawned. Almost immediately she yawned back and delivered a cup of coffee to his table.

"How do you feel?" he asked, his hand deliberately brushing hers.

"Tired. How about you?"

"Exhausted. I'm not used to these late nights and early mornings." His hand continued to hold hers, his thumb stroking the inside of her wrist.

"And you think I am?" she teased.

His eyes widened for an instant. "Can I see you tonight?"

The thought of refusing wasn't within her. "Depends." No need to let him feel overconfident. "What do you have in mind?" She batted her eyelashes at him wickedly.

"Collecting on what's due me. Eight, I believe, is the correct number."

Chapter Four

The half-moon silently smiled down from the starlit heavens, casting its golden shadow over the sandy beach. Breed and Peter had gathered some driftwood, and blue tongues of fire flickered out from between the small, dry logs.

Elizabeth sat in the sand beside the fire and leaned against Breed's quiet strength. His arms were wrapped around her from behind, enclosing her in his wide embrace. His breathing was even and undisturbed in the peace of the night. Communicating with words wasn't necessary. They'd been talking all week, often into the early hours of the morning. Now, words seemed unnecessary.

"I love this beach," Elizabeth murmured, thinking how easy it would be to close her eyes and fall asleep in Breed's arms. "Ever since the first night you brought me here I've come to think of this beach as ours."

His hold tightened measurably as he rubbed his jaw over the top of her head, mussing her wind-tossed hair all the more. Gently he lowered his head and kissed the side of her neck. "I'd say we're being more than generous sharing it with the world, wouldn't you?"

Elizabeth snuggled deeper into his arms. "More than generous," she agreed.

The sound of Gilly's laughter could be heard drifting down the beach. Gilly and Peter had taken off running in a teasing game. Elizabeth enjoyed it when the four of them did things together, but she was grateful for this time alone with Breed by the fire.

"Where do they get their energy?" Elizabeth asked, having difficulty restraining a wide yawn. "I don't know about you, but I can't take another week like this."

"I meant to get you home earlier," Breed murmured, his voice faintly tinged with guilt.

They'd gone out every night, and Elizabeth hadn't gotten to bed before midnight any one of those evenings. Each time they promised one another they'd make it an early evening, but they hadn't met that goal once. The earliest Elizabeth had crawled into bed had been twelve-thirty. Even then, she'd often lain awake and stared at the blank ceiling, thinking how dangerously close she was to falling in love with Breed.

"I wish I knew more about the constellations," she whispered, disliking the meandering trail of her thoughts. Love as an emotion between two people had often troubled her. Elizabeth had never known what elusive qualities distinguished love from infatuation.

And if she did convince herself she was in love with Breed, would she ever be certain that it wasn't gratitude for the renewed lease on life he had so unwittingly given her? Tonight, in his arms, she could lie back and stare at the stars blazing in the black velvet sky. Only weeks ago she would have stumbled in the dark, unable to look toward the light. Breed had fixed that for her.

A hundred times Elizabeth had flirted with the idea of telling him who she was. Each time, she realized that the knowledge would ruin their relationship. She'd be faced with leaving him, Gilly, and San Francisco soon enough.

She recognized that it was selfish to steal a few weeks of happiness at the expense of others, but Elizabeth couldn't help herself. It'd been so long since she'd felt this good. Without even knowing it, Breed and Gilly had given her back the most precious gift of all—the ability to laugh and see beyond her grief. Being with them had lifted her from the mire of regret and self-pity. For that she would always be grateful.

"What's wrong?" Breed asked, tenderly brushing the hair from her temple.

His sensitivity to her moods astonished Elizabeth. "What makes you ask?"

"You went tense on me for a moment."

Elizabeth twisted so that she could lean back and study Breed's ruggedly powerful face. His eyes were shadowed and unreadable, but she recognized the disquietude in his look. Something was troubling Breed. Elizabeth could sense it as strongly as she could feel the moisture off the ocean mist on her face. She'd recognized it in his eyes several times this past week. At first she'd thought it was her imagination. A yearning to understand Breed overcame her. "Things aren't always what they appear," she found herself saying. She hoped that he trusted her enough to tell her what was troubling him. But she wouldn't force his confidence.

Everything seemed to become still. The sound of the waves pounding against the beach faded. "What makes you say that?"

Elizabeth resumed her position, disappointed and a little hurt. If Breed had secrets, so did she, and she certainly wouldn't blurt out her circumstances. In all fairness, she shouldn't expect him to.

"Nothing." Her low voice was filled with resignation.

Slowly, tantalizingly, Breed ran his hands down her arms. "I'm going to be out of town a couple of days next week."

"Oh." The one word trembled on her lips with undisguised disappointment.

"I'll be flying out Monday, but should be back sometime Tuesday afternoon," he explained.

"I'll miss you."

His arms drew her back against the unrestrained strength of his torso. "I wouldn't go if it wasn't necessary. You're right, you know." He spoke so low that Elizabeth had to strain to hear him. "Things aren't always what they appear."

Later, when Breed had dropped her off at the apartment and Elizabeth had settled in bed, Breed's enigmatic words echoed in her mind. She couldn't imagine what was troubling him. But whatever it was, she sensed he was planning to settle it while he was out of town. He'd been quiet tonight. At first she had attributed his lack of conversation to how tired they were. But it was more than that. She didn't know any other way to explain it.

When she had first met Breed she'd seen him as muscular and handsome, two qualities she had attributed to shallow and self-centered men. But he had proved her wrong. This man was deep and intense. So intense she often wondered what it was that accounted for the powerful attraction that had brought them together.

A shadowy figure appeared in the doorway. "Are you asleep?" Gilly whispered.

Elizabeth sat up, bunching the pillows behind her back. "Not yet." She gestured toward the end of her bed, inviting her roommate to join her.

Gilly took a long swallow from a glass of milk and walked into the moonlit room, sitting on the edge of the bed. "I don't know what's wrong. I couldn't sleep either."

"Did you have a good time tonight?" Elizabeth felt compelled to ask in a whisper, although there was no one there whom she could wake.

"I enjoy being with Peter," Gilly confessed on an exaggerated sigh, "but only as a friend."

"Is that a problem?"

Gilly's laugh was light and airy. "Not really, except that I'm sure he feels the same way. It makes me wonder if I'll ever fall in love."

Elizabeth bit into her lip to keep from laughing out loud. "Do you realize how funny you sound? First you're happy because Peter feels the same way about you. Then you're disappointed because you aren't in love."

Gilly's smile was outlined by the filtered light of the moon passing through the open window. "Yes, I suppose it does sound a little outrageous. I guess what I'd really like is to have the kind of relationship you and Breed share."

"He's a special man." Elizabeth spoke wistfully. Breed had taught her valuable lessons this past week. Without her long walk in the valley she may not have recognized the thrill of the mountaintop. Breed and Gilly had taught her to laugh and love again. Life was beautiful in San Francisco. No wonder her mother had loved this city.

"I've seen the way Breed looks at you," Gilly continued, "and my heart melts. I want a man to feel that way about me."

"But not Peter."

"Peter, Fred, John. At this point I'm not choosy. I want to know what it's like to be in love. Really in love, like you and Breed."

"In love? Me and Breed?" Elizabeth tossed back the words in astonished disbelief.

"Yes, you two," Gilly returned indignantly. "You mean you didn't know?"

"You've got this all wrong." Elizabeth's thoughts were waging a fierce battle with one another. Gilly had to be mistaken. Breed couldn't be in love with her. She could hurt him. The minute he learned about her wealth and position, he would feel betrayed and angry. Intense feelings for one another would only complicate their relationship, and she couldn't allow that to happen. "We're attracted, but we're not in love," she returned adamantly, nodding her head once for emphasis.

The sound of Gilly's bemused laugh vibrated across the room. "Honestly, how can anyone be so blind?"

"But Breed and I hardly know one another," Elizabeth argued. "What we feel at this point are kindred spirits. Infatuation, maybe, but no one falls in love in two weeks."

"Haven't you read *Romeo and Juliet*?" Gilly asked her accusingly. "People don't need a year's courtship to know they're in love."

"Breed's a wonderful man, and I'd consider myself fortunate if he loved me." A thickening lump tightened her throat, making it impossible to talk for a moment. "But it's too soon for either of us to know what we really feel. Much too soon," she reiterated.

Gilly was uncharacteristically quiet for a long moment. "Maybe I'm all wet," she murmured thoughtfully. "But I don't think so. I have the feeling that once you admit what's going on inside your heart and your head, you won't be able to deny it."

"Perhaps not," Elizabeth murmured, troubled by Gilly's words.

"Are you seeing him tomorrow?"

"Not until the afternoon. Breed decided that, after all the sleep I lost this week, I should sleep in the morning."

"But you're awake because you're lying here thinking about him. Right?" Gilly asked softly.

"No." Elizabeth yawned loudly, raising her arms high above her head. She hoped her friend would take the not-so-subtle message.

"And not being able to sleep doesn't tell you anything?" Gilly asked again.

"It tells me that I'd have a much easier time if a certain know-it-all wasn't sitting on the end of my bed, bugging the heck out of me." As much as she wanted to deny her friend's assessment, Elizabeth had been impressed more than once with Gilly's insight into people and situations. The twenty-year-old was wise beyond her years.

"I can take a hint, unlike certain people I know," Gilly said, bounding to her feet and feigning outrage. "You wait, Elizabeth Wainwright, when you realize you're in love with Breed your head's going to spin for a week."

"Probably." Turning onto her side, she scooted down and pulled the covers over her shoulders. "But don't count on it," she mumbled into the pillow, forcing her eyes closed.

Standing beside the foot of the bed, Gilly finished the rest of her milk. "I'll see you in the morning," she said as she headed toward the door.

"Gilly." Elizabeth stopped her. "Breed's not really in love with me, is he?"

Staring pointedly at the ceiling, Gilly slowly shook her head in undisguised disgust. "I swear the girl's blind," she said to the light fixture. "Yes, Breed's head over heels in love with you. Only a fool wouldn't have guessed. Good night, fool."

"Good night," Elizabeth murmured with a sinking feeling. She'd been naive to believe that she could nurture this relationship with Breed and not pay any emotional price. She had to do something soon—before it was too late. If it wasn't already.

"All right," Breed said, breathing heavily. He tightened his grip on Hilda's steering wheel. "Out with it."

Elizabeth's face paled as she glanced out the side of the Jeep. The afternoon had been a disaster from the start. She had hoped to speak honestly with Breed. She wanted to tell him that she was frightened by what was happening between them. At first she'd thought to suggest that Breed start seeing someone else, but the thought of him holding another woman had made her stomach tighten painfully. The crazy part was that she'd never thought of herself as the jealous type.

"Are you pouting because I'm going to be away for a few days? Is that the reason for the silent treatment?"

"No," she denied in a choked whisper. "That's not it." She kept her face averted, letting the wind whip the honey curls in every direction. She was so close to tears it was ludicrous.

When Breed pulled over to the side of the street and parked, Elizabeth's heart sank to her knees. A gentle hand on her shoulder was nearly her undoing. She didn't want him to be gentle and concerned. If he were angry it would be so much easier to explain her confused thoughts.

"Beth, what is it?"

Like Gilly, Breed had started calling her Beth. But it wasn't what he called her, it was the way he said it, the tender, almost loving way he let it roll from his lips. No name had ever sounded so beautiful.

Miserable, Elizabeth placed her hand over his and turned around so that she could see his face. Of their own volition, her fingers rose to trace the angular planes of his proud jaw.

He emitted a low groan and took hold of her shoulders, putting distance between them. "I have enough trouble keeping my hands off you without you doing that."

Elizabeth dropped her hands, color rushing to her cheeks. "That's what's wrong," she said in a low voice she hardly recognized as her own. "I'm frightened, Breed."

"Of what?"

Elizabeth swallowed at the uneasiness that filled her. "I'm worried that we're becoming too intense."

Breed dropped his hands and turned so that he was staring straight ahead. As if he needed something to do with his fingers, he gripped the steering wheel. Elizabeth could tell that he was angry by the way his knuckles paled. His look proved he didn't understand what she was saying.

"Things are getting too hot and heavy for you. Is that it?"

It wasn't, but she didn't know how else to explain her feelings. "Yes...yes they are."

"Then what you're saying is that you'd prefer it if we didn't see each other anymore?"

"No!" That thought was intolerable.

"The trouble with you is that you don't know what you want." The icy edge to his tone wrapped its way around Elizabeth's throat, choking off a reply.

Breed didn't appear to need one. Without hesitating, he turned the ignition key, and Hilda's engine roared to life. Jerking the gearshift, he pulled back onto the street.

"I feel we both need time to think." She shouted to be heard above the noise of the traffic. Breed didn't answer. Before Elizabeth could think of another way to explain herself, Breed had pulled up in front of the brick apartment building. He left the engine running.

"I agree," he said, his voice emotionless, "we've seen too much of one another."

"You've misunderstood everything I've said," she murmured miserably, wishing she had explained herself better.

"I don't think so," he replied, his jaw tightening. "I'll call you Tuesday afternoon when I get back to town. That is, if you want to hear from me again."

"Of course I do." She'd forgotten about his trip. Frustration rocked her. "I regret having said anything. I don't want you to go away angry."

He hesitated, and although he didn't say anything for several moments, Elizabeth could feel the resentment fade. The air between them became less oppressive, lighter. "The thing is, you're right," he admitted tightly. "Both of us needed to be reminded of that. Take care of yourself while I'm away."

"I will," she whispered.

"I'll phone you Tuesday."

"Tuesday," she agreed, climbing out of the car. She stood on the sidewalk as Breed pulled away and merged with the flowing traffic.

A flick of her wrist turned the key that allowed her into the apartment. Gilly sat on the sofa, reading a romance novel and munching on a carrot when Elizabeth entered the apartment. "How did everything go?"

"Fine," Elizabeth responded noncommittally. But she felt miserable. Her talk with Breed hadn't settled anything. Instead of clearing the air, it had only raised more questions. Now she was left with three days to sort through her thoughts and decide how she could continue to see Breed and not complicate their relationship by falling in love.

"If everything's so wonderful, why do you look like you're going to burst into tears?"

Elizabeth tried to smile, but the effort failed miserably. "Because I will."

"I take it you don't want to talk."

It was all Elizabeth could manage to shake her head.

Later that evening, as the sun was sinking low into a lavender sky, Gilly dressed for an evening out. Her cousin was getting married, and Gilly's parents expected her to attend the wedding although Gilly claimed she never had cared for this particular cousin.

"Are you sure you won't come?" Gilly asked Elizabeth for the sixth time.

"Not this time," Elizabeth responded, making an exaggerated stroke along the side of her nail with the file. Fiddling with her fingernails had given the appearance she was busy and untroubled. But Elizabeth doubted that her smoke screen had fooled Gilly. "I thought you'd conned Peter into going with you."

"I regret that," Gilly said with frank honesty.

"Why?" Elizabeth glanced up from the kitchen table where she sat with a collection of nail polish.

"Knowing my dad, he's probably going to make a big deal about my bringing Peter. This whole thing's going to end up embarrassing us both. I hate being forced to attend something just because it's family."

Elizabeth cast her a sympathetic look. She'd suffered through enough family obligations to empathize with her friend's feelings.

Gilly and Peter left soon afterward, and Elizabeth finished her nails, wondering if Breed would notice when she saw him next. Television entertained her for a time, keeping her mind off Breed. But not for long.

Picking up the paperback novel Gilly had been reading, Elizabeth scanned the first couple of chapters, surprised at how much she was enjoying the book. The next thing she knew, Gilly was shaking her awake and telling her to climb into bed or she'd get a crick in her neck. Elizabeth couldn't recall having drifted asleep.

It was the middle of the morning when she woke again. Feeling out of sorts and cranky, Elizabeth read the morning paper and did the weekly grocery shopping. When Gilly suggested a drive, Elizabeth declined. Not until later did she realize that she'd been waiting for Breed to phone and was keenly disappointed when he didn't.

Monday evening when the phone did ring she all but flew across the room in her eagerness to answer. She desperately wanted it to be Breed. But it wasn't. Instead, she found herself talking to her disgruntled father.

"I haven't heard from you, dear. Are you okay?"

"Of course I am." Although disappointment coated her voice, Elizabeth had to admit she was pleased to hear from her father. She was even more grateful that Gilly was taking a shower and wasn't likely to overhear the conversation. "I'm happy, Dad, for the first time since Mom died."

"I was thinking about this job of yours. Are you still working as a...waitress?" He said the word as though he found it distasteful.

"Yes, and I'm enjoying it."

"I've been talking to some friends of mine," her father said in a dignified tone that told her he was anxious about her. "If you feel you need to work, then we could get you on at the embassy. Your French is excellent."

"Dad," Elizabeth interrupted, "I like it at the Patisserie. Don't worry about me."

"But as a common waitress?" The contemptuous disbelief was back in his voice again. "I want so much more for you, Princess." Her father hadn't called her that since she was thirteen. "When are you coming home? I think it might be a good idea if you were here."

"Dad!" Elizabeth wailed impatiently. "For the first time in months, I'm sleeping every night. I'm eager for each new morning. I'm happy, really happy. Don't ruin that."

She could hear her father's uncertainty, feel his indecision. "Have you met someone important?" he said.

The question was a loaded one, and Elizabeth wasn't sure how to respond, especially in the light of her discussion with Breed. "Yes and no."

"No one important?" he pressed.

"I've made some friends. Good friends. What makes you ask?"

"No reason. I just don't want you to do something you'll regret later."

"Like what?" Indignation caused her voice pitch to rise perceptibly.

"I don't know." He paused and exhaled forcefully. "Siggy's phoned for you several times."

Elizabeth released an inward groan. Siegfried Winston Chamberlain III was the most boring stuffed shirt she'd ever known. More than that, Elizabeth had openly disliked Siggy from the day a small, helpless bird had flown into a freshly washed window and broken its neck. The look in Siggy's eye revealed that he'd received enjoyment in witnessing its death. From that time on she'd avoided him. But Siggy had pursued her relentlessly from their teenage years. Elizabeth was convinced he wasn't in love with her. She wasn't even sure he liked her. What she did recognize was the fact that a union between their two families would be financially expedient to the Chamberlains.

"Tell Siggy the same thing you told him when I was in Paris."

"Siggy loves you."

"Dad." Elizabeth didn't want to lose her patience, not on the phone when it would be difficult to settle their differences. "I honestly don't think Siggy knows what love is. I've got to go. I'll phone you next week. Now, don't worry about me. Promise?"

"You'll phone next week?"

Elizabeth successfully repressed a sharp reply. Her father had never shown such concern for her welfare. He was acting as though she was working undercover for the CIA.

Honestly! Elizabeth mused irritably. Would she ever understand her father?

"You miss him, don't you?" Gilly questioned later that evening.

Elizabeth didn't even try to pretend. She knew Gilly was referring to Breed. He had been on her mind all weekend. Monday had dragged and she was counting the hours until she could see him again. "I do," she admitted readily. "I wish I'd never said anything."

Gilly nodded sympathetically. Elizabeth had confided in her friend and was again grateful for Gilly's insight and understanding.

But it was more than missing Breed, Elizabeth thought to herself. Much more. For three days it had been as though a vital part of her had been missing. The realization frightened her. Breed had come to mean more to her in a few weeks than anyone she'd known. Gilly, too. As she'd explained to her father, she was making friends. Maybe the first real friends of her life. But Breed was more than a friend, and it had taken this separation to prove it.

Tuesday Elizabeth sat by the phone.

"If you sit any closer to that telephone, someone might think you're waiting for a call," Gilly teased.

"Am I that obvious?"

"Is the sun bright? Do bees buzz?" Gilly sat on the chair opposite Elizabeth. "Why not call him? Women do that these days, you know. He may even be waiting to hear from you."

Elizabeth hesitated long enough to consider the idea. "I don't know."

"Well, it isn't going to hurt anything. You were the one who suggested this separation. His pride's been bruised. You've been open with him to this point. Besides, anything's better than having you mope around the apartment another night."

"I do not mope."

Gilly tried unsuccessfully to disguise a smile. "If you say so."

Elizabeth waited until nine for Breed to phone. She could call him, but seeing him in person would be so much better. Maybe Gilly was right and he was waiting for her to contact him. She wouldn't sleep tonight unless she made the effort to see him. It wouldn't do any good to try and fool herself.

"I think I'll go for a walk," Elizabeth announced brightly, knowing she wasn't fooling her friend.

"The night's perfect for a stroll," Gilly murmured, not taking her eyes from the television, but Elizabeth noticed the way the corners of her eyes crinkled as she struggled not to reveal her amusement. "I don't suppose you want me to wait up for you."

With a bemused smile, Elizabeth closed the door, not bothering to answer her friend.

There could be several reasons why Breed hadn't called. Maybe his trip had been extended. He might not even be home. But as Gilly had pointedly stated, the evening was perfect for a stroll. The sun had set into a cloudless horizon and darkness had blanketed the city. The streets were alive with a variety of people. Elizabeth didn't notice much of what was going on around her. Her quick, purpose-filled strides took her the three blocks to Breed's apartment in a matter of a few short minutes.

For all her resolve, when she saw the light under his door, her heart sank. Breed was home and hadn't contacted her.

Her first light knock went unnoticed, so she rang the doorbell, pressing into the buzzer long and hard.

"Beth." Breed sounded shocked when he opened the door.

"So you made it back safely after all," she said, aware of the faintly defensive note in her voice. He must have realized that she would be waiting for his call. "What time did you get back?" The minute the question slipped from her lips, she regretted having asked. Her coming was obvious enough.

"About six." He stepped back, silently and grudgingly issuing the invitation for her to come inside.

She was surprised at how bare the apartment looked. The living area displayed nothing that stamped the apartment with Breed's personality. There were no pictures on the walls or books and magazines lying around. The apartment seemed sterile, it was so clean. It looked as if he'd just moved in.

"I thought you said you would phone."

"I wasn't sure you wanted to hear from me."

Without waiting for an invitation, Elizabeth sat on the sofa and crossed her long legs, hoping to give a casual impression.

Breed took the chair on the other side of the room. He leaned forward, his elbows resting on his knees. There was a coiled alertness about him that he was attempting to disguise. But Elizabeth knew him too well. In the same way that he was sensitive to her, she was aware of him. He seemed to be waiting for her to speak.

"I missed you," she said softly, hoping her words would release the tension in the room. "More than I ever thought I would."

Breed straightened and looked uncomfortable. "Yes. Well, that's only natural. We've been seeing a lot of one another the last couple of weeks."

Her fingers were laced together so tightly that they began to ache. She unwound them and flexed her hands before standing and moving to the window on the far side of the room. "It's more than that," she announced with her back to him. Deliberately she turned, her hands resting on the windowsill. "Nothing seemed right without you...."

Breed vaulted to his feet. "Beth, listen to me. We're tired. It's been a long day. I think we should both sleep on this." His look was an odd mixture of tenderness and impatience. Hurried strides took him into the kitchen, where he picked up a sweater that was folded across a chair. "Come on, I'll drive you home."

"No." She knew a brush-off when she saw one. Breed didn't want her here; that much was obvious. He hadn't been himself from the moment she set foot in the door. "I walked here; I'll walk back."

"All right, I'll come with you." The tone of his voice told her he'd brook no argument.

She lifted one shoulder in a half-shrug. "It's a free country."

Breed relaxed the minute he locked the door. There was something inside the apartment he hadn't wanted her to see; Elizabeth was sure of it. He wouldn't have a woman hiding in his bedroom; Elizabeth wouldn't believe that. Amusement must have drifted across her face in a slow smile.

"What's so funny?" Breed wanted to know.

"Nothing."

His hand gripped hers. "Come on, and I'll introduce you to BART."

Elizabeth paused midstride, causing Breed's step to falter slightly. With her hands positioned challengingly on her hips, she glared defiantly at him. "Oh, no you don't, Andrew Breed. If you don't want to see me again, then fine. But I won't have you introducing me to other men. I can find my own dates, thank you."

A crooked smile slashed his face as he turned toward her, his eyes hooded. "Bay Area Rapid Transit. BART is the subway."

"Oh." Elizabeth felt ridiculous. The natural color of her cheeks was heightened with embarrassment.

"So you missed me," Breed said casually as they strolled along the busy sidewalk. "That's nice to know."

Elizabeth greeted his words with silence. First he had shunned her and now he was making fun of her. Other than a polite "good night" when they arrived at her building, she didn't have anything to say to Breed. The whole idea of going to him had been idiotic. Well, she'd learned her lesson.

"The thing is, I discovered I missed you too."

Again Elizabeth didn't respond.

"Missing someone is a funny thing," Breed continued. "There are varying degrees. Like after your mother died, I imagine..."

Elizabeth felt a chill rush over her skin that had nothing to do with the light breeze. "I never told you my mother was dead," she said stiffly.

Chapter Five

You don't mind, do you?" Gilly asked contritely. "I wouldn't have mentioned your mother to Breed if I'd known you objected.

"No, don't worry about it," Elizabeth said gently, shaking her head.

"You have to remember," Gilly continued, "that Breed and I went out several times before you started dating him."

Elizabeth had forgotten.

"I knew from the beginning that Breed was really interested in you," Gilly went on. "From the first date you were all he talked about."

Breed had explained yesterday that Gilly had told him about Elizabeth's mother. Yet she'd doubted him. Everything about last night remained clouded in her mind. From the moment she'd entered his apartment, Elizabeth had felt like an unwelcome intruder. None of his actions made sense, and her suspicions gave her a feeling of paranoia.

"Tonight Peter and I are going to dinner and a movie," Gilly reminded Elizabeth.

"I have some shopping I want to do," she returned absently.

Not until later that afternoon when Elizabeth faced the store detective did she remember that she couldn't phone Gilly and have her come. A heaviness pressed against her heart, and she struggled to maintain her composure as the balding man led her toward the department store office.

Elizabeth walked past the small crowd that had gathered near her and saw a tall, familiar figure on the far side of the floor in the men's department.

"Breed," she called, and she all but ran to him, thanking God that he had chosen this day to shop.

He turned at the sound of her voice, his brow thickened. "Beth, what is it?"

She bit into her bottom lip, more embarrassed than she could ever remember being. "Someone stole my purse. I haven't got any way to get home or a key to the apartment."

Elizabeth's face was buried in her hands when Breed delivered a steaming cup of coffee to the kitchen table where she sat. The manager had let her into the apartment, adding another humiliation to her ordeal.

"Tell me again what happened," Breed said as he straddled a chair beside her.

Elizabeth shook her head. Everything important was inside her purse. Her money, credit cards, identification. Everything. Gone in a matter of seconds. As crazy as it sounded, Elizabeth felt as if she personally had been violated. Nothing this terrible had ever happened to her. She felt both stunned and angry.

"I don't want to talk about it," she replied stiffly. What she wanted was for Breed to leave so she could be alone. Venting some of the outrage would help ease the hard knot in the pit of her stomach.

"Beth." He said her name so gently that she closed her eyes to the emotion it wrought within her. "Honey, I can't help unless I know what happened."

One tear broke over the thick dam of her lashes and flowed unrestrained down her pale face. Resolutely, she wiped it aside.

"I decided to do a little shopping after work. Peter had picked up Gilly and they were going out, and I didn't want to go home to an empty house." Breed hadn't mentioned anything last night about getting together, and she didn't want to sit around in an empty apartment on a beautiful afternoon.

"Go on," he encouraged. His hand continued to hold hers, his thumb stroking the inside of her wrist in a soothing action that at any other time would have been sensuous and provocative.

"I'd only bought a couple of things and decided to stop in the rest room before taking the bus home. I set my purse and the packages on the counter while I washed. I turned to dry my hands on a paper towel. When I turned back, my purse, the packages...everything was gone. I was so stunned I didn't know what to do."

"You must have seen something."

"That's what Detective Beaman thought. But I didn't. I didn't even hear anything." She paused, reliving the short second. She could tell them nothing.

Even now, an hour later, sitting in her kitchen, a feeling of disbelief filled her. This couldn't really be happening. This ordeal was a bad dream and when she woke everything would be fine again. At least that was what Elizabeth desperately wanted to believe.

"What did they take?"

"Breed, don't. Please. I can't talk about it anymore. I just want to take a bath and pretend this never happened." Later she'd be forced to contact her father. It didn't take much of an imagination to know what his response was going to be. He'd insist she leave San Francisco, and they'd argue. Elizabeth let the unpleasant thoughts fade. She didn't want to think about it.

Breed released her wrist and stood. His hands were positioned on his lean hips, his expression grim and unyielding. "Beth," he insisted in a low, coaxing tone. "Think. There's something you're not remembering. Something small. Close your eyes and go over every minute of the time you were shopping."

Elizabeth clenched her teeth to keep from yelling. "Don't you think I haven't already?" she said with marked impatience. "Every detail of every minute has been playing back repeatedly in my mind."

Breed exhaled sharply, his action letting her know his patience was as limited as her own.

Elizabeth stared pointedly at the bare surface of the table which blurred as the welling tears collected in her eyes. She managed to restrain their fall, but she couldn't keep her chin from trembling. Tears were a sign of weakness, and one the Wainwrights frowned upon.

A sigh came from Breed as he eliminated the distance between them and stood behind her. Gently his hands comforted her by massaging her shoulders and neck. The demanding pressure of his fingers half lifted her from the chair, forcing her to stand.

Elizabeth held herself stiff and angry. "This is your fault" she whispered in a faintly hysterical tone.

"Mine?" Breed turned her around. His wide, muscular chest rose in deep breaths and his amber eyes narrowed into thin slits.

Elizabeth didn't need him to tell her how unreasonable she was being. Her tears blurred his expression as she lashed out at him bitterly. "Why were you so unwelcoming last night? Why didn't you want me at your apartment yesterday?" She inhaled shakily. "Don't bother to deny it. I'm not stupid. I know when I'm not wanted. And why...why didn't you come into the café today?" Her accusations were fired as quick as machine gun bullets.

Breed groaned as his hands cupped her face. The anger that flashed across his features had vanished. "There wasn't a single minute that you weren't on my mind." A thick furrow of self-derisive anger darkened his face.

"Then why..." Her heart fluttered uncertainly, excited and yet afraid.

Motionless, he held her, revealing none of his thoughts. "Because," he admitted as a smouldering light of desire burned in his eyes. His hand slid slowly along the back of her waist, bringing her infinitesimally closer.

When he fitted his mouth to hers, a small, happy sound escaped from her throat. His thick arms around her waist lifted her from the kitchen floor. Her softness was molded to his male length as he kissed her until her lips were swollen and trembling.

"I missed you so much," Elizabeth cried, wrapping her arms around his neck. "I was so afraid you didn't want to see me again."

"Not want to see you?" he repeated. His husky tone betrayed his frustration. "You confuse me. I don't know what kind of game you're playing."

Anxiously, she brushed the hair from his face and kissed his eyes, her lips exploring the planes and contours of his angular features with short, teasing kisses. "I'm not playing any game," she whispered happily.

Breed loosened his grip so that her feet touched the floor once again. "No games?" Amusement was carved in the lines of his face. "I don't believe that."

Deliberately she directed his mouth to hers and kissed him long and slow, her lips moving sensuously over his.

Breed broke the contact and held her away at arm's length as he took in several deep breaths.

"What's wrong?" she whispered. She didn't want Breed to pull away from her. A chill seeped through her bloodstream as she tried to decipher his attitude. The messages he sent her were confused. He wanted to be with her, but he didn't. He liked coming to her apartment, but didn't want her at his. His kisses affected her as much as they affected him, yet he pulled away whenever their lovemaking became too intense.

The phone rang, and Breed dropped his hands and stared at it as if it were an intruder. "Do you want me to answer it?" he questioned.

Elizabeth shook her head, indicating she would answer it. "Hello." She couldn't disguise the soft tremble in her voice. "Yes, yes, this is Elizabeth Wainwright."

Breed brushed his fingers through his hair as he paced the area in front of the phone.

"Yes, yes," Elizabeth repeated breathlessly. "I did lose my purse." Not until the conversation was half over did the words sink into her consciousness.

"Breed," she cried excitedly as she replaced the receiver. "They've found my purse."

"Who?" He turned her in his arms, his tense features relaxing.

"The store. That was them on the phone. Apparently whoever took it was only after the cash. Someone turned it into the office only a few minutes ago after finding it in the stairway."

"Your credit cards and identification?"

"There. All they took was the cash."

Breed hauled her into his arms and released a heavy sigh that revealed his relief. Her own happy sigh joined his. "They said I should come and pick it up. Let's go now," she said, laughing. "I feel naked without my purse." Giddy with relief, she waltzed around the room until Breed captured her and swung her in the air as if she weighed no more than a play doll.

"Feel better?"

"Oh, yes," she exclaimed, kissing him lightly. "Can we go now?"

"I think we should." He laced their hands together, then lifted their clenched fists to his lips and kissed the back of her hand.

Breed locked the apartment with the key the manager had given her and tucked it into his pocket. Hand in hand they walked outside.

Elizabeth patted Hilda's cushion. "You know what I thought last night?" she asked as Breed revved the engine.

Breed turned and smiled warmly at her. "I can't imagine." His finger lingered longer than necessary as it removed a long strand of silken hair that the wind blew across her happy face.

"For one fleeting instant, I was convinced you were hiding a woman in your bedroom." At the shocked look Breed gave her, Elizabeth broke into delighted giggles.

"Beth." Thick lines marred his smooth brow. "Whatever made you suspect something like that?"

Pressing her head against his shoulder, she released a contented sigh. "I don't know." She did know, but she wanted to relish this moment. Yesterday's ghosts were buried. Today's happiness shone brightly before her. Her joy was complete. "Forward, Hilda. Take me to my purse."

Breed merged with the heavy flow of traffic. "I suppose you're going to insist on celebrating."

"Absolutely."

"Dinner?"

Elizabeth sat up and placed her hand on his on the gearshift. She had to keep touching him to believe that all this was real. "Yes, I'm starved. I don't think I've eaten all day."

"Why not?" He gave her a questioning sidelong glance.

She poked his stomach. "You know why."

Breed's hand claimed hers, and again he kissed her fingers. Elizabeth had the sensation he felt exactly as she did and couldn't keep his hands off her.

"What did Beaman say?"

"It wasn't Beaman. He said his name, but I can't remember it now."

"What did he say?" Breed glanced briefly in her direction.

"Just that the store would be closing in a few minutes and we should come right away."

"You should come right away." He drawled the words out slowly. Then he dropped her hand and tightened his hold on the steering wheel as he glanced in the rearview mirror. The tires screeched as he made a U-turn in the middle of the street. The unexpected action caused Hilda to teeter for an instant.

"Breed," Elizabeth screamed, holding onto the padded bar on the console. "What is it? What's wrong?"

He didn't answer her as he weaved in and out of the traffic, blaring his horn impatiently. When they pulled in front of the apartment, Breed looked around and tensed.

Elizabeth had no idea what had gotten into him. "Breed." She tried a second time to talk to him. He sat alert and stiff. The look in his eyes was frightening. She had never seen anything more menacing.

"Call the police," he told her as he jumped from the Jeep.

"But, Breed."

"Now, damnit, and hurry."

Confused, Elizabeth climbed onto the street. "What am I supposed to tell them?" she cried as she followed him onto the sidewalk and reached for his hand.

Carelessly Breed threw her arm free. "That wasn't the store that called," he explained impatiently. "But whoever took your purse."

"How do you know?" Nothing made sense anymore. Breed was like a dangerous stranger. Rage contorted his features until she hardly recognized him.

He took her with his hands, his fingers biting mercilessly into her shoulders. "Look." He jerked his head to the moving van that was parked in front of the building. "Now go do as I say," he ordered in a threatening voice. "And don't come into the apartment until after the police arrive. Now go."

"Breed." Panic filled her as he walked toward the building. "Don't go in there," she shouted frantically, running after him. He was so intent that he didn't hear her. His glance of surprise was quickly replaced with an angry scowl. "Get out of here."

With fear dictating her actions, Elizabeth ran across the street to a beauty shop. She was sure the women thought she was crazy when she grabbed the phone, dialed the emergency police number, and reported a robbery in progress.

Like a caged animal, Elizabeth paced the sidewalk outside the apartment waiting for the patrol car. She held both hands over her mouth as she looked up and down the street. Everything was taking so long. Each second was an hour. Every minute a lifetime. Not until the first police vehicle pulled up did Elizabeth realize how badly she was trembling.

"In there," she said, and she shouted her apartment number. "My boyfriend went up to stop them."

Another police car arrived, and while one officer went into the building the other stayed outside and questioned Elizabeth. At first she stared at him blankly, her mind refusing to concentrate on even the uncomplicated responses. Her answers were clipped, one-word replies.

Fifteen minutes later, two men and a woman were led out of the building by the police. Breed followed, talking to an officer. He paused long enough to search out Elizabeth in the growing crowd and smile reassuringly.

Her answering smile was shaky, but she felt her heart regain its normal rhythm. Her eyes followed him as he spoke to one officer and then another. When he joined her a few minutes later, Breed slipped an arm around her waist with familiar ease. Her fears evaporated at his touch.

"Do you recognize any of them?" he asked her.

Lamely, she nodded. "The woman was in the elevator with me, but she didn't go into the rest room."

"But she got off on the same floor?"

Elizabeth wasn't sure. "I don't remember, but she must have."

"It doesn't matter if you remember or not. There's enough evidence here to lock them up." His arm remained on her waist as he directed her inside the building.

"How'd you know?" Dazed and somewhat tongue-tied, she stared up at him. "What clued you in to what was going on?"

"To be honest, I don't know," Breed admitted. "Something didn't ring true. First it wasn't Beaman who phoned and then there was something about the way you were instructed to come right away. They were probably waiting outside the building within sight and saw us leave."

"But how'd they know my address and phone number?" All her identification listed her Boson address. Even her driver's license was from Massachusetts. There hadn't been any reason to obtain a California license, since she didn't have a car and was only planning on staying the summer months.

"Your name, address, and telephone number are printed on the outside of your checkbook."

Elizabeth groaned. "Of course."

"We need to go to the police station and fill out a few forms. Are you up to that?"

"I'm fine. But I want to know about you. What happened in there?"

"Nothing much." He didn't look like he wanted to talk about it. "I counted on the element of surprise."

"Yes, but there were three of them against you." Elizabeth wouldn't let the subject drop so easily. "How did you defend yourself?"

His wide shoulders tensed as he hesitated before answering. "I've studied the martial arts."

"Breed!" she exclaimed. "Really? You should have said something." The longer she was with Breed the more Elizabeth realized how little she actually knew about him. Many of these subjects were ones she had avoided, afraid of revealing too much about herself. But she wouldn't shy away from them anymore.

Oblivious to the afternoon's happenings, Gilly and Peter returned to the apartment chatting happily.

Elizabeth glanced up and sighed. "Where were you when I needed you?" she teased her roommate.

"Why, when did you need me?"

"Today. Someone took my purse."

"Took," Breed repeated with a trace of anger. "We foil a sting operation and she defends these creeps."

"Sting operation." Peter looked incredulous. "I think you better start at the beginning."

Slowly, shaking her head, Elizabeth sighed. "Let me explain."

An hour later, Breed glanced pointedly at his wristwatch and held out his hand to Elizabeth. "Walk me to the door." The quiet firmness of his request and the tender look in his eyes sent her pulse racing.

"Sure," she said, eagerly moving around the sofa to his side.

Breed waited until they were just inside the entryway to turn her into his arms. Her back was supported by the panels of the door. His hands were on each side of her head as his gaze roamed slowly over her upturned face. For one heart-stopping second his eyes rested on her parted lips; his look was as potent as a physical touch.

"I want to see you tomorrow."

Elizabeth released a heavy sigh. "Oh, thank goodness," she said, offering him a brilliant smile. "I was afraid I was going to be forced to ask you out."

His look grew dark and serious. "You'd do that?"

"Yes." She didn't trust herself to add an explanation.

He pulled his gaze from hers. "Would you like to go fishing?"

"You mean with poles and hooks and worms?"

"I've got a sailboat. We could leave tomorrow afternoon, once you're free."

"Can I bring anything?"

"The worms," Breed teased.

"Try again, fellow. How about some sandwiches?" She could have Evelyn make some up for her before she left the Patisserie tomorrow.

"Fine."

Breed's kiss was disappointingly short, but immeasurably sweet. Long after he left, Elizabeth felt his presence linger. Twice she turned and started to say something, before realizing he'd left for the evening.

Elizabeth felt Gilly's curious stare as she came out of the bedroom the following afternoon.

"Where's Breed taking you, for heaven's sake? You look like something out of Li'l Abner."

Self-consciously, Elizabeth looked down at her tennis shoes and the faded jeans that were rolled midway up her calf. The shirttails of the red-checkered blouse were tied loosely at her midriff.

"Fishing. I'm not overdressed, am I? My swimsuit's on underneath this."

"You look..." One side of Gilly's mouth quirked upward as she paused, her face furrowed in concentration. "Different," she concluded.

"I'll admit I don't usually dress like this, but..."

"It's not the clothes," Gilly interrupted. "I thought that at first, too. But that's not it. There's a certain aura about you. A look in your eye."

Turning, Elizabeth found a mirror and examined herself closely. "You're crazy. I'm no different than I was last week, or last night for that matter."

Gilly ignored her and paid excessive attention to the crossword puzzle she was doing.

"Aren't you going to comment?" Elizabeth asked mockingly. She was used to doing verbal battle with her roommate.

Gilly bit into the eraser at the tip of the pencil. "Not me. I learned a long time ago that it's better not to argue with you." But she rolled her eyes when she thought Elizabeth wasn't looking.

Breed picked her up a couple of minutes later, and Elizabeth didn't have the opportunity to banter with Gilly further. If there was something different about her, as her friend believed, then it was because she was happier, more complete.

Walking outside the building, Elizabeth scanned the curb for Hilda, Breed's lovable old Jeep. But it wasn't parked within sight.

"Here." Breed held open the door to a silver sedan.

"Where's Hilda?"

"Home." Breed's reply was abrupt.

"Good grief, how many cars have you got?"

The smile that pulled up the edges of his mouth looked forced. "One too many," he answered cryptically.

Elizabeth wanted to question him further, but he closed her door and walked around to the driver's side. He paused and glanced at the street before climbing inside the car.

"Are you planning on kidnapping me?" she teased.

For an instant his sword-sharp gaze pinned her against the seat. "What makes you ask something as crazy as that?" Impatience sounded in his crisp voice.

Elizabeth had meant it as a joke, but Breed had taken her seriously. She arched one delicately shaped brow at his defensive tone and cocked her head. "What's gotten into you?"

"Nothing."

Releasing her breath slowly, Elizabeth gazed out the side window, watching as the indistinguishable scenery whipped past. From the minute Breed had asked her on this outing, she had been looking forward to their time together. She didn't want anyone or anything to ruin it.

At the marina, Breed's heavy steps sounded ominously as he walked the long wooden walkway that led to his moored sailboat. But his mood altered once they were slicing through the water, the multicolored spinnaker bloated with wind. Content, Elizabeth dragged her fingers in the darkish green waters of San Francisco Bay, delighting in the cool feel against her hand.

"This is wonderful," she shouted. But Breed couldn't hear her as a gust of wind carried her voice forward. Laughing, that they could be sitting beside one another and not hear, Elizabeth scooted closer, rose to her knees, and spoke directly into his ear.

Breed's returning smile revealed his own enjoyment. He relaxed against the gunnel, his long legs stretched out and crossed at the ankles. One hand managed the tiller and he motioned with the other for Elizabeth to sit at his side.

She did so willingly.

When Breed reached a spot that apparently met his specifications, he lowered the sails and dropped anchor.

Giving her nothing more than the basic instructions, he baited Elizabeth's hook and handed her a fishing pole.

"Now what?" She sat straight-backed and unsure as Breed readied his pole and lowered the line into the deep waters on the opposite side of the boat.

"We wait for a hungry fish to come along and take a nibble."

"What if they're not hungry?"

"Are you always this much trouble?" he asked her, chuckling at her indignant look. "Your freckles are flashing at me again."

Involuntarily a hand brushed her nose as though her fingers could rub the tan flecks away. She was about to make a feisty retort when she felt a slight tug on her line.

"Breed," she whispered frantically. "I...I think I've got one." The pole dipped dramatically, nearly catching her off guard. "What do I do?" she cried, looking back to him, her eyes wild and unsure.

"Reel it in."

"I can't," she cried, silently pleading with him to take the pole from her. She should have known better than to ask.

"Sure you can," he assured her calmly. To grant her moral support, Breed reeled in his line, encouraging her as she struggled to reel in the fish.

Elizabeth couldn't believe how much of a battle one small fish could give. "What have I caught," she shouted in her excitement, "a whale?" Perspiration broke out across her brow as she pulled back on the pole and reeled in the fish inch by inch.

When the line snapped and she staggered backward, Breed caught her at the shoulders. "You all right?"

"No, damnit, I wanted that fish. What happened?"

Breed looked unconcerned, and he shrugged. "Any number of things. Want to try again?"

"Of course," she replied indignantly. Breed seemed to think she was a quitter. Fine. She'd like nothing better than to prove him wrong.

With her line back in the bay, Elizabeth leaned against the side, lazily enjoying the sun and wind. "Have you ever stopped to think that after all the times we've gone out that we hardly know anything about one another?" she queried.

Her statement was met with silence. "What's there to know?"

She was treading on dangerous ground, and she knew it. Her relationship with Breed had progressed to the point where she felt he had a right to know who she was. But fear and indecision prevented her from broaching the subject boldly. "There's lots I'd like to know about you."

"Like what?" There was the slightest pause before his mouth thinned. Breed didn't seem overly eager to reveal more of himself.

"Well, for one thing...your family." If she led into the subject, then maybe he'd ask her about hers and she could explain bits and pieces of her background until things added up in his mind. Telling him outright could be fatal to a promising relationship.

"Not much to tell you there. I'm the oldest of four boys. My great-grandfather came to California from Germany in search of lumber. He died here and left the land to his son." He paused and glanced at her. "What about you?"

She pressed her lips tightly together. For all her desire for honesty, when it came time to reveal her family she found she couldn't. The bright, healthy color the wind and the sun had given her cheeks was washed swiftly away, leaving her unnaturally pale.

"I've got one older brother, Charlie." She swallowed tightly. "I don't think you'd like him."

"Why not?"

She lifted one petite shoulder. "He's...well, he's something of a stuffed shirt."

"Lawyer type."

She nodded, wanting to change the subject. "How much longer before I lure another fish to my bait?"

"Patience, little one, patience," Breed said, his back to her.

Elizabeth fluttered her eyes closed. Her heart was pounding so hard she was sure Breed would notice. Unwittingly, Breed had given good advice. She had to be patient. Someday soon she'd tell Breed everything.

Chapter Six

The starts were twinkling like diamond chips in an ebony sky. The water lapped lightly against the side of Breed's boat. The sailboat, with sails lowered, rocked gently in the murky water of San Francisco Bay. Four pairs of eager eyes gazed into the night sky anticipating the next rocket burst to explode into a thousand shooting stars that briefly lit up the heavens.

"I love the Fourth of July," Elizabeth murmured. Breed sat beside her, his arm draped casually over her shoulder. Gilly and Peter sat on the other side of the boat, holding hands. The two were obviously not in love, but as Gilly explained, they were good friends.

One burst after another brightened the sky for a few seconds. Breed had said something earlier that week about going to Candlestick Park to watch the fireworks display. But once the four piled into Breed's sedan they discovered that the traffic heading for the park was horrendous. Consequently, Breed suggested that they take his sailboat into the bay and observe the fireworks from there. The idea had been met with enthusiasm from the other three.

For nearly a week Breed had taken Elizabeth on his boat every night after work. Sometimes they fished, depending on how much time they had and what their plans were afterward. Breed had let her crawl forward a couple of times to raise and lower the sails. Elizabeth loved to sail as much as Breed. The time they shared on the water had become the high point of her day. They talked openly, argued over politics, discussed books. Breed challenged her ideas on conservation and pollution, forcing Elizabeth to stop and think about things she had previously accepted because of what she'd been told by others. Gently, but firmly, Breed made her form her own opinions. And she loved him for it.

She hadn't told Breed she loved him. The emotion was new to her and frightened her a little. The love she'd experienced in the past for her family and friends had been a mixture of respect and admiration. The only person with whom she had ever shared such a close relationship in the past had been her mother. Of course, she would have grieved if her father had been the one who had suffered the stroke and died. But her mother had been her soulmate.

The love she felt for Breed went beyond friendship. Her love was fiery and intense, and the physical desire was sometimes overwhelming. Yet the joy she felt in his arms exceeded desire. Yes, she wanted him. More than that, she wanted to give herself to him. Breed must have known that, but he never allowed their lovemaking to go beyond a certain point. She didn't know why he was holding himself back. Not that Elizabeth minded; this aspect of their relationship was only a small part of her feelings. When they could speak openly and honestly about their feelings and their commitment to one another, then they could deal with that aspect of their relationship. Her love went so much deeper. In analyzing her feelings, Elizabeth thought that they also met on a deeper plane, a spiritual one. Perhaps Breed felt it was too soon to talk about these things. In some ways, they didn't need to.

Often Elizabeth had wanted to talk to Gilly about her feelings, but she was certain Gilly wouldn't understand. If her mother had been alive, Elizabeth could have spoken to her. But she wasn't, and Elizabeth was forced to keep this inexplicable intensity of human relationships buried deep within her heart.

The only thing that marred Elizabeth's happiness was the sensation that something was troubling Breed. She'd tried to question him once, and ran up against a granite wall. Lately he'd been brooding and thoughtful. Although he hadn't said anything, Elizabeth was fairly certain he'd lost his job. His hours had been flexible in the past, but lately he'd been coming into the Patisserie at all hours of her shift. Some days he'd arrive in the morning and come again in the afternoon. Another thing she'd noticed was that they rarely ate in restaurants anymore. All the things they did together were inexpensive. Every Sunday they returned to Sigmund Stern Grove for the free concert. They took long walks on the beach and sailed almost daily. Breed's money problems created others. The situation effectively killed her desire to tell him about her background. She couldn't tell him about her family's money. Elizabeth had no doubt that the information could ruin what they shared.

When Elizabeth glanced up from her musings, she noted that Peter's arm was around Gilly and that she had her head pressed against his shoulder. The look in Gilly's eye was troubled, although Elizabeth could have misread it in the reflected moonlight.

"Gilly, are you feeling okay?" Elizabeth felt obliged to ask.

Gilly straightened. "Of course. Why shouldn't I be?"

"You're so quiet."

"I think we should enjoy the novelty," blond-haired Peter interjected. "Once ol' motor-mouth gets going, it's hard to shut her up."

"Motor-mouth," Gilly returned indignantly, poking Peter between his ribs with her finger. Peter laughed and the joking resumed, but not before Elizabeth witnessed the pain in her friend's expression.

An hour later, Elizabeth helped Breed fold up the sails after docking. Gilly and Peter carried the picnic basket and blankets to the car.

"Something's bothering Gilly," Elizabeth murmured to Breed the minute her friend was out of hearing distance.

"I noticed that too," Breed whispered conspiratorially. "I think she's falling in love with Peter."

"No." Elizabeth shook her head decisively. "They're just good friends."

"It may have started out like that, but it's not that way anymore." He sounded completely confident. He hardly paused as he moved forward in the boat to store the sails.

Elizabeth followed him aboard. It pitched as she placed her weight against the stern. "What makes you so sure Gilly's in love?"

A weary look stole across his features. "She has that look about her." From his tone, Elizabeth could tell he didn't want to discuss the subject further.

"And apparently you've seen that look in a lot of women's eyes," she stated teasingly with a serious undertone.

"A few," he responded noncommittally.

The thought of Breed's loving another woman produced a curious ache in her heart. Elizabeth paused and straightened, placing a hand over her breast. *So this is jealousy*, she mused. This churning sensation in the pit of her stomach, this inexplicable pain in her chest. As crazy as it seemed, she was jealous of some nameless other woman.

Breed's hand at her elbow brought Elizabeth back to the present. He took her hand as he stepped onto the dock. "Peter and Gilly are waiting."

The silence coming from the backseat of the car where Gilly and Peter were sitting was heavy and unnatural. A storm cloud seemed to have settled in the sedan, the air heavy with electricity. Breed captured Elizabeth's gaze and arched his brows in question.

She motioned weakly with her hand, telling him she hadn't any more of an idea of what had happened between Peter and Gilly than he did. Twice Elizabeth attempted a conversation, but her words were met with uninterested grunts.

Breed pulled up and parked in front of the girls' apartment, and he was helping Elizabeth out when Gilly practically jumped over the backseat.

"'Night, everyone," she said in a voice that was high-pitched and wobbly.

"Gilly, wait up. I want to talk to you." Peter bolted after her, his eyes filled with frustration. He cast Breed and Elizabeth an apologetic look on his way past.

Breed glanced at Elizabeth and shrugged his shoulders. "I'd say those two need some time alone."

"I agree."

"Do you want to go for a drive?" Breed suggested, tucking her hand against his folded arm as he led her back to the sedan.

"How about a walk instead? After sailing in the boat all evening, I could use some exercise."

Breed turned her in his arms. "We could. But I'd rather drive up to Coit Tower and show you the city lights. The view is fabulous."

Spending time alone with Breed was far more appealing than watching the city lights. "I'd like that," she admitted, climbing inside the car.

The long, winding drive through the dense neighborhood led to the observation tower that was situated high above the city. Breed hadn't exaggerated the view. Elizabeth had seen some of the most beautiful landscapes in the world, but sitting with Breed overlooking San Francisco, she couldn't recall one more beautiful. Words couldn't describe the wonder of what lay before her.

"It's late," Breed murmured against her hair.

Elizabeth acknowledged his words with a short nod, but she didn't want to leave and didn't suggest it.

"You have to work tomorrow." His voice was rough and soft, more of an aching whisper.

A smile touched Elizabeth's eyes. Breed couldn't decide if they should stay or go. Alone in the dark with nothing to distract them, the temptations were too great.

Elizabeth tipped her head back. "Let me worry about tomorrow. I'll survive," she assured him. The night shaded his eyes, but she could feel the tenseness about him. His breathing was faintly irregular. "Why do you want to leave so much?" she asked in a throbbing whisper.

Her question went unanswered. A long moment of silence followed as he gazed down on her. Gently, his fingers brushed the wispy strands of hair from her cheek, then curled into her hair. Elizabeth was shocked to realize he was trembling.

Slowly his head moved downward and paused an inch above her lips. "You know why we should leave," he growled.

All day she had yearned for him. Not for the first time, Elizabeth noticed that Breed had been physically distant, his touch casual, as though he was struggling to hold himself back. His restraint made her want him all the more. They were playing with dynamite, and like an inquisitive child Elizabeth wanted to discover more, regardless of the danger.

"Beth." He whispered her name and something snapped within him. His mouth plundered hers, twisting against hers as they were swept on the crest of a crashing wave. All her senses came to life, and she rose slightly from the seat to press closer to him. When his hands fumbled with the buttons of her shirt, she arched her back to grant him easier access. His hands felt like coals of fire as they cupped the undersides of her soft breasts and he buried his face in their fullness.

A tiny moan slipped from her as his lips found her neck and shot wave after wave of sensual delight through her. Elizabeth's hands roamed from his back and unfastened his shirt. Eagerly her hands glided down the smooth flat muscles of his broad chest.

Breed groaned and straightened. He buried his face in her neck and held her to him. "Beth," he moaned. "Don't move." She could feel and see the conflict in his eyes. He was trapped between his desire and his conscience.

"Don't move? Why?" she asked in surprise, her voice warm and trembling.

He released one hand to rub across his face and eyes, but he held her tightly to him with the other as though he couldn't bear to release her yet.

"You know why," he told her. His control was almost frightening. The marvel of it silenced her for several seconds.

With her arms linked behind his head, Elizabeth pressed her forehead to his. "Yes, I know why," she whispered.

The tension eased from his muscles, and she could hear the uneven thud of his heart slowly return to normal. When his breathing was less ragged, she lightly pressed her lips to his.

"Don't do that," he said harshly, releasing her abruptly. The violence in him was barely suppressed.

She turned from him and pressed her head against the back of the seat, staring straight ahead. When tears of anger and frustration filled her eyes, she blinked hurriedly to forestall their flow.

"There's only so much of this a man can take." He stared straight ahead and savagely rubbed his hand along the back of his neck. "You know as well as I do what's happening between us."

"I can't help it, Breed," she whispered achingly.

"Yes, you can," he returned grimly.

The ache to reach across the close confines of the car and touch him was unbearable. But she knew she dare not. She couldn't look at him. "Is...is there something physically wrong with me?" she asked in a tortured whisper. "I mean, do my freckles turn you off...or something?" Out of the corner of her eye, Elizabeth saw a muscle twitch in his lean jaw.

"That question isn't worthy of an answer." His eyes hardened as he turned the ignition key and revved the engine, snapping it into gear.

"Maybe we should stop seeing so much of one another." Her pride was hurt, but the ache extended deep within her heart.

He didn't answer her until they were into the city. "Maybe we should," he said at last.

Elizabeth closed her eyes to the onrush of emotional pain. One tear escaped and made wet tracks down her pale face, followed by another and another.

When Breed arrived at her apartment building she didn't make a pretense of bidding him good night. She didn't want him to see her tears. That would only humiliate her further.

"Thanks for a lovely day," she whispered, unable to find her voice, and she hurriedly opened the door, racing into the apartment foyer.

Breed didn't follow her, but he didn't leave either. His car was still parked outside when Elizabeth reached her apartment. From deep within the living-room shadows she glanced out the window to watch him. The streetlight silhouetted a dejected figure of a man leaning over the steering wheel.

Soft, whimpering cries could be heard coming from the bedroom. Trapped in her own problems, Elizabeth had forgotten Gilly's.

Wiping the moisture from her cheek, she turned and headed down the hall to knock against her friend's open bedroom door.

"Gilly," she whispered. "What's wrong?"

Gilly sat up in the twin bed and blew noisily into a tissue. "Beth, I am so stupid."

"If you want to talk, I have all the time in the world to listen." Elizabeth came into the darkened room and sat on the end of the bed. With all the problems she was having, she chastised herself for not recognizing what had been happening to her friend.

Gilly took another tissue and wiped her eyes dry. "Do you remember I told you that Peter and I are just friends?"

"I remember."

"Well..." Gilly sniffled noisily, "something changed. I don't know when or why, but sometime last week I looked at Peter and I knew I loved him."

Elizabeth patted Gilly's hand. "That's no reason to cry. I'd think you'd be happy."

"I was, for two glorious days. I wanted to tell someone, but I didn't think it was fair to confide in you. Peter should be the one to know."

Her roommate had appeared exceptionally happy lately, Elizabeth recalled. Gilly had been enthusiastic about the four of them spending the holiday together. The difference in her attitude had been difficult to pinpoint, because Gilly was always happy.

"Then I made the mistake of telling Peter," she continued. "You were helping Breed put the sails away and Peter and I were carrying things to the car." Gilly inhaled a quivering breath.

"What happened?" Elizabeth encouraged her roommate softly.

"I guess I should have waited for a more appropriate moment, but I was eager to talk to him. Everything about the day had been perfect. And we were alone for the first time. So, like an idiot I turned to him and said, 'Peter, I don't know what's happened, but I love you.'"

"And?"

"First he looked shocked. Then embarrassed. He stuttered something about this being a surprise and looked like he wanted to run away, but you and Breed returned and we all piled into the car."

"What happened when Breed dropped the two of you off here?" Elizabeth wanted to know.

"Nothing. I wouldn't talk to him."

"Gilly!"

"You wouldn't have wanted to talk either," she cried, defending her actions. "I was humiliated enough without Peter apologizing to me because he didn't share my feelings."

"I'm sure he's going to want to talk to you." Elizabeth appealed to the more reasonable part of her friend's nature.

"He can forget it. How could I have been so stupid? If I was going to fall in love, why couldn't it be with someone like Breed?"

Elizabeth lowered her gaze to her hands. "There's only one Breed, and he's mine."

"Oh, before I forget." Gilly sat up and looked around her, finally handing Elizabeth a piece of paper with a phone number written across the top. "Your brother phoned."

"My brother? From Boston?"

"No, he's here in San Francisco. He's staying at the Saint Francis. I told him I didn't know what time you'd be back, so he said to tell you that he'd expect you tomorrow night for dinner at seven-thirty at his hotel."

Ordering instead of asking; it sounded just like her brother.

"Did he say anything else?" It would be just like Charlie to say something to embarrass her.

Gilly shook her head. "Not really, except..."

"Yes?" Elizabeth stiffened.

"Well, your brother's not like you, is he?"

"How do you mean?" Elizabeth queried.

"I don't know exactly. But after I hung up I wondered if I should have curtsied or something."

After a single telephone conversation, the astute Gilly had her brother pegged. "He's like that," Elizabeth admitted.

"Well, anyway, I gave you the message."

"And I'll show up at the hotel and hope I use the right spoon or my dear brother will be outraged."

For the first time that evening Gilly smiled.

The café hadn't been open for more than five minutes when Breed strolled in and sat at his regular table. Elizabeth caught sight of his broad shoulders the moment he entered the Patisserie. Even after all these weeks her heart stirred at the sight of him, and now it throbbed painfully. One part of her wanted to rush to him, but she resisted.

Carrying the coffeepot, she approached his table. Breed turned over the ceramic mug for her.

"Morning," she said as unemotionally as possible.

"Morning," he echoed.

Her eyes refused to meet his, but she could feel his gaze concentrating on her. "Would you like a menu?"

"No, just coffee."

She filled his cup.

"We need to talk," Breed announced casually as his hands folded around the light brown cup.

Elizabeth blinked uncertainly. "I can't now," she replied nervously. "Mornings are our busiest time."

"I didn't mean now." The words were enunciated slowly, as if the control on his patience had been stretched to the limit. "Tonight, when we're able to discuss things freely, would be better, don't you think?"

Elizabeth hedged, shifting her weight from one foot to the other. "I can't," she murmured apologetically. "My brother's in town, and I'm meeting him for dinner."

His level gaze darted to her, his eyes disbelieving.

"It's true," she declared righteously. "We're meeting at the Saint Francis."

"I believe you."

Frustrated, Elizabeth watched as a hard mask stole over his face. "You have dinner with your brother."

"I wasn't waiting for your approval," Elizabeth remarked angrily.

His amber eyes blazed for a furious second. "I didn't suppose you were."

Indecision made her hesitate. She wanted to turn and present him a clear view of her back, yet at the same time she wanted things right between them. The harmony they'd shared so often these past days was slowly disintegrating before her eyes.

"Would you care to join us?" The question slipped from her naturally, although her mind was screaming for him to refuse.

"Me?" Breed looked aghast. "You don't mean that."

"I wouldn't have issued the invitation otherwise." The entire evening would be a disaster. Elizabeth could imagine Charlie's reaction to someone as large and muscular as Breed.

Breed appeared to give her invitation some consideration. "No," he said, and Elizabeth couldn't prevent the low but controlled breath of relief. "Maybe another time."

"Do you want to meet later?" she asked, and her voice thinned to a quavering note. "Dinner shouldn't take long," she said, glancing down at her practical white shoes. "I want to talk to you too."

"Not tonight." The lines about his mouth deepened with growing impatience. Although she'd asked him to join her and Charlie, she realized that Breed knew she didn't want him there. "I'll give you a call later in the week." He stood, and with supple strides left the café.

Elizabeth watched him go and had the irrational urge to throw his untouched coffee after him. That arrogant male pride of his only fueled her anger.

That night Elizabeth dressed carefully in a raspberry-colored dress with a delicate white miniprint. A dress that would meet with Charlie's approval, she mused as she examined herself in the mirror. Not until it was time to go did she stop to consider why he was in town. The family had no business holdings on the West Coast. At least none that she knew about. She hoped he hadn't come to persuade her to return to Boston. She'd just about made up her mind to make San Francisco her permanent home. The city was lovely, and the thought of leaving Breed was intolerable. She wouldn't leave the man she loved.

The taxi delivered her to the entrance of the prestigious hotel at precisely seven-ten. The extra minutes gave her the necessary time to compose herself. She was determined to make this a pleasant meeting. A confrontation with her brother was the last thing she wanted.

"Lizzy."

Elizabeth groaned inwardly. Only one person in the world called her that.

"Hello, Siggy." She forced herself to smile and extended her gloved hand for him to shake. To Elizabeth's acute embarrassment, Siggy pulled her into his arms and kissed her soundly. Her mouth was opened in surprise, and Siggy seemed to assume she was eager for his attention and deepened the kiss.

Without making a scene, Elizabeth was left to endure his deplorable touch.

The sound of someone clearing his throat appeared to bring Siggy back to his senses. He broke the contact, and it was all Elizabeth could do not to rub the feel of his mouth from hers with the back of her hand. Siggy's touch made her skin crawl, and she glared angrily from him to her brother.

"There are better places for such an intimate greeting," Charlie Wainwright said, slapping Siggy across the shoulder. "I told you she'd be happy to see you."

Siggy ignored Elizabeth's brother. "It's good to see you, Lizzy."

Elizabeth was unable to restrain the involuntary grimace. "Don't call me Lizzy," she said between clenched teeth.

"It's a term of affection," Charlie inserted, glancing at his slim gold watch. "Our table should be ready. Names are something I'll leave for you two to discuss later."

Later. She cringed at the thought. There wasn't going to be a later with Siggy. Not if she could prevent it. Now she understood why Charlie had come to San Francisco; he wanted to foist Siggy on her. Charlie would be the one to profit most from a marriage between the two families. She hadn't realized it at the time, but Charlie mentioned Siggy at every opportunity lately. That was the reason she'd found herself avoiding her brother. His selfishness made her want to cry.

By some miracle, Elizabeth was able to endure the meal. She spoke only when a question was directed to her and smiled politely at appropriate intervals. The knot in her throat extended all the way to her abdomen and felt like a rock in the pit of her stomach. The two men discussed Elizabeth at length, commenting several times on how good she looked. Charlie insisted she would make a radiant bride and declared that their father would be proud of her, knowing she had chosen so well. Charlie made the marriage between her and Siggy sound like a foregone conclusion and one that had been endorsed wholeheartedly by her father. Questions buzzed around Elizabeth's head like irritating bees. In the past she'd had her differences with her father, but he wouldn't do this to her. She had to believe that. Yet her father had mentioned Siggy during their last few telephone conversations.

Resignedly, Elizabeth followed her brother and Siggy to her brother's suite at the suggestion of an after-dinner drink.

The small glass of liqueur helped chase the chill from her slender frame. Siggy sat on the plush sofa beside Elizabeth and draped his arm possessively around her shoulder. She found his touch suffocating, and she pointedly removed his arm and scooted to the other side of the sofa. Undaunted, Siggy followed.

"I can see that you two have a lot to discuss," Charlie said, exchanging knowing smiles with the younger man. Without another word, he excused himself and left Elizabeth alone to deal with Siggy. The moment the door clicked closed, Siggy was on her like a starving man after food.

Pinned against the corner of the couch, Elizabeth jerked her face left and right in an effort to avoid his punishing kiss.

"Siggy," she gasped, pushing him off her. "Stop it."

Composing himself, Siggy sat upright and made a pretense of straightening his tie. "I'm sorry, Lizzy. It's just that I love you so much. I've wanted you for years, and now I know that you feel the same way."

"What?" she exploded.

"Lizzy, my sweet, darling Lizzy." Siggy brushed a stray hair from her flushed cheek. "Charlie told me how you've had this crush on me for years. Why didn't you say something? You must have known how I feel about you. I've never made any secret of that."

A lump of outrage and shocked disbelief grew in her breast. Charlie had maliciously lied to Siggy. Words of explanation were trapped in her lungs. Her own brother had sold her for thirty pieces of silver. She was nothing more to Charlie than the means of securing a financial coup that would link the two families. His own selfish interests were paramount.

"Where is my brother?" Elizabeth managed finally. "I'd like to talk to him."

"He'll be back," Siggy said as he stood, crossed the room, and helped himself to another glass of brandy. "He wanted to give us some time alone. Want some, darling?" He held up the brandy and eyed her solicitously.

"No." Irritated, she shook her head. "And...and what would happen to the two companies once...once our families were linked."

Smug and secure, Siggy silently toasted her. "A merger. It's the financial feat of the year, Charlie says. My family will give Charlie the exclusive contract for distribution of our stores. Already we're planning expansion within a three-state area."

Momentarily shocked, Elizabeth felt tears form in her eyes. It was little wonder that Charlie was doing this. A lucrative contract with Siggy's family department store was something the Wainwrights had sought for years. But the price for Elizabeth was far too high.

Charlie returned a few minutes later, looking pleased and excited.

"If you'll excuse us a minute, Siggy," Elizabeth said bluntly, "I'd like to talk to my brother alone."

"Sure." Siggy glanced from brother to sister before setting his drink aside. "I'll be in the lounge when you're finished."

The second the door clicked closed, Elizabeth whirled on her brother. "How could you?" she demanded.

Charlie knotted his fists at his sides. "Listen, little sister, you're not going to ruin this for me. Not this time."

"Charlie, I'm your only sister. How could you ask me to marry a man I don't love? A man I don't even respect..."

Charlie's mouth tightened grimly. "For once in your life, stop thinking of yourself."

"Me?"

"Yes, yes." He paced the floor in short, angry strides. "All right, I admit I went about this poorly, but marrying Siggy is what mother would have wanted for you."

"That's not true." Her mother knew her feelings about Siggy and would never have pressured her into something like this.

"What do you know?" He hurled the words at her furiously. "You only thought of yourself. You never knew what mother was really thinking. It was your selfishness that killed her."

The blood drained from Elizabeth's face. Elizabeth and her mother had spent the afternoon shopping and, not feeling well, her mother had gone to lie down before dinner. Within an hour she was dead, a victim of a massive stroke. In the back of her mind, Elizabeth had carried the guilt that something she had done that day had caused her death.

"Charlie, please," she whispered frantically. "Don't say that. Please don't say that."

"But it's true," he shouted. "I was with father when the doctor said that having you drag her from store to store was simply too much. It killed her. You killed her."

"Oh, dear God." Elizabeth felt her knees buckle as she slumped onto the sofa.

"There's only one thing you can do now to make up for that, Elizabeth. Do what mother would have wanted. Marry Siggy. It would have made her happy."

He was lying; in her soul, she knew he was lying. But her own flesh and blood, her only brother whom she had loved and adored in her youth, had used the cruellest weapon in his arsenal against her. With hot tears scalding her cheeks, Elizabeth stood, clenched her purse to her breast, and walked out the door.

She didn't stop walking until she found a taxi. Between breathless but controlled sobs she gave the cabbie her address. Not until he pulled away from the curb did Elizabeth realize how badly she was shaking.

"Are you all right, lady?" The cabbie looked at her anxiously in the rearview mirror.

Elizabeth couldn't manage anything more than a nod.

When they arrived in front of her apartment, Elizabeth handed him a twenty-dollar bill and didn't wait for the change. Not wanting Gilly to see her, she hurried in the door.

"You're back soon." The sound of the television drifted from the living room.

"Yes," Elizabeth mumbled, keeping her head turned and lowered, not wanting her friend to see the tears. She continued walking. "I think I'll take a bath and go to bed."

Gilly must have looked up for the first time. The sound of her surprised gasp was like an assault, and Elizabeth flinched. "Elizabeth. Good grief, what's wrong?"

"Nothing." Elizabeth looked at the wall. "I'm fine. I just need to be alone." She went into the bedroom and closed the door, leaning against it. Reaction set in, and she started to shake uncontrollably. Fresh tears followed. Tears of anger. Tears of hate. Tears of pain and pride.

Softly Gilly knocked on the closed bedroom door, but Elizabeth ignored her. She didn't want to explain. She couldn't; not when she was crying like this. Maybe later she could make up some excuse. She fell into the bed and curled in a tight ball in an attempt to control the freezing cold that made her shake so violently.

When she inhaled a quivering sob, she heard Gilly talking to someone. Her friend's voice was slightly high-pitched and worried. Elizabeth felt guilty that she was worrying Gilly like this, but she couldn't help it. Later she would make up some excuse. But she couldn't now.

Five minutes later there was another knock on her door. Elizabeth ignored it.

"Beth," the voice said softly. "Open up. It's Breed."

"Breed," she sobbed, throwing back the covers. "Oh, Breed." She opened the door and fell into his arms, weeping uncontrollably. Every part of her clung to him as he lifted her into his arms and carried her into the living room.

With an infinite gentleness he set her on the couch and brushed the hair from her face.

"Good Lord." Breed paused and stiffened. "Who did this to you?"

Chapter Seven

Elizabeth was crying so hard that she couldn't have answered. Nor did she know how to explain. She didn't want to tell Breed and Gilly that the brother she loved had betrayed her in the worst possible way.

Breed said something to Gilly, but Elizabeth didn't hear. "Beth," he whispered, removing her fingers from his shoulders as he sat beside her, half lifting her onto his lap. "Tell me what's upset you like this?"

Forcefully, she shook her head and inhaled deep breaths that became quivering sobs until she regained control of herself. Crying like this was only making matters worse.

That terrible, crippling pain of Charlie's betrayal was there in her eyes and she couldn't do anything to conceal it. A nerve twitched in Breed's hard, lean jaw, his features contorted, and pain showed clearly in his eyes. Her pain. She was suffering, and that caused him to hurt as well. Elizabeth couldn't have loved anyone more than she did right at that moment. She didn't know what Breed believed happened, and she couldn't utter a word to assure him.

"I'm fine. No one hurt me...physically," she said in a trembling voice she barely recognized as her own. "Just hold me." She had trouble trying to control her breathing. Her body continued to shake with every inhalation.

"I'll never let you go," Breed promised as his lips moved against her hair. She felt some of the tenseness leave him and felt his relief that things weren't as bad as he'd thought.

Warm blankets were wrapped around her, so warm they must have recently been taken from the dryer. That was what Breed had asked Gilly to do, Elizabeth realized now.

He continued to talk to her in low, soothing tones until her eyes drifted closed. Caught between sleep and reality, Elizabeth could feel Breed gently free himself from her embrace and lay her on the sofa. A pillow cushioned her head and warm blankets surrounded her. She didn't know how long Breed knelt beside her, smoothing her hair from her face, his touch so tender she felt secure and protected. Gradually a calmness surrounded her, and Elizabeth knew she was on the brink of falling asleep. Breed left her side. He had told her he wouldn't leave, and she was comforted just by knowing he was in the same room.

"All I know," Elizabeth heard Gilly whisper, "was that she was meeting her brother for dinner. What could he have done to cause this?"

"You can bet I'm going to find out," Breed stated in a dry, hard voice that was frightening in its intensity.

"No." Elizabeth struggled to a sitting position. "Just drop the whole matter. It's my own affair."

Breed's eyes narrowed.

"Elizabeth," Gilly murmured with wide, worried eyes, "I've never seen you like this."

"I'm fine, really." She brushed back the wet strands of hair. "I'm just upset. I apologize for making a scene."

"You didn't make a scene," Gilly returned soothingly.

Breed brought her a damp cloth and, kneeling at her side, gently brushed it over her cheeks. It felt cool and soothing over her hot face. His jaw was clenched and pale, as if he couldn't stand to have her hurt in any way, physically or emotionally.

Taking her hand, Elizabeth rubbed the side of his face and pulled him to her, wrapping her arms around his neck. "Thank you."

"For what? I should have been there for you."

"You couldn't have known." It wasn't right that Breed should accept any blame for what had happened.

Breed took her hands and gently raised them to his mouth and kissed her knuckles. "Beth." His eyes implored hers. "I want you to trust me enough to tell me what happened tonight."

She lowered her gaze and shook her head. "It's done. I don't want to go over it again."

The pressure on her fingers was punishing for a quick second. "I'll kill anyone who hurts you like this again."

"That's exactly why I won't say."

The tension between them was so palpable that Elizabeth could taste it. Their eyes clashed in a test of wills. Unnerved, she lowered hers first. "I need you here," she whispered in a soft plea. "It's over now. I want to forget it ever happened."

Gilly hovered close. "Do you feel like you could drink something? Tea? Coffee? Diet Pepsi?"

The effort to smile was painful. "All I want is a hot bath and bed." Her muscles ached, and she discovered that when she stood, her legs wavered unsteadily and she leaned against Breed for a moment.

Gilly hurried ahead and filled the bathtub with steaming, scented water. Next she brought in fluffy, fresh towels.

"You want me to stay in the bathroom while you bathe, don't you?" Breed asked, and a crooked smile slanted his mouth. The humor didn't quite touch his eyes, but Elizabeth appreciated the effort.

"No. If I need anyone, Gilly can help."

"Pity," Breed grumbled.

The hot water helped relieve the aching tension in her muscles. Even now her body was coiled and alert. Her temple throbbed less and the pain in her heart had receded. As she rested against the back of the tub, Elizabeth's mind kept running over the details of the evening, but she forced the painful images to the back of her mind. She didn't feel strong enough emotionally to deal with it now. Maybe tomorrow.

Gilly stayed with her, more on Breed's insistence than because she felt Elizabeth needed her. Together they emerged from the steam-filled bathroom. Breed led Elizabeth into her room. The sheets on her bed had been folded back, and her weak smile silently thanked him.

"You won't leave me?" Her eyes pleaded with him as he tucked in the covers.

"No," he whispered. "I said I wouldn't." His kiss was so tender that fresh tears misted her eyes. "Go to sleep," he whispered encouragingly.

"You'll be here when I wake up?" She needed that reassurance.

"I'll be here."

The dark void was already pulling her within its welcoming arms. As she drifted inside, Elizabeth could hear Breed's low voice quizzing Gilly.

The sound of someone obviously trying to be quiet and not succeeding woke Elizabeth. The room was dark, and she glanced at her clock radio to note that it was just after three. She sat up in bed and blinked. The memory of the events of the evening pressed heavily against her heart. Although she was confident Charlie would never have abandoned her to Siggy if her brother had known what Siggy was capable of doing, the sense of betrayal remained. To try to push her off on Siggy was deplorable enough. Slipping from between the sheets, she put on her silk housecoat and moved into the living room.

"Hello, twinkle-toes," she whispered to Breed, not wanting to disrupt Gilly's sleep.

"Did I wake you?" Breed sat up and wiped a hand across his weary face. The sight of him trying to sleep on the couch was ludicrous. His feet dangled far over the end, and he looked all elbows and arms.

"You wake me? Never. I thought an elephant had escaped and was raging through the living room."

His smile was evident in the moonlight. "I got up to use the bathroom and walked into the lamp," he explained with a chagrined look.

"It was selfish of me to ask you to stay," she said, sitting down beside him.

"I would have stayed whether you asked me to or not." He reached for her hand and squeezed it gently. "How do you feel?"

She shrugged and lowered her gaze to her knees. "Like a fool. I don't usually overreact that way."

"I know," Breed murmured. "That's what concerned me most." He put his arm around her, and she rested her head against his shoulder. "Sometimes the emotional pain can be twice as bad as anything physical." She murmured on a long, drawn-out yawn. "When you love and trust someone and they hurt you, then the pain goes beyond anything physical." While relaying the details of what had happened, Elizabeth was explaining the situation to Breed. He'd asked her to trust him, and she did. It was important that he realize that.

Breed didn't comment, but she felt him stiffen slightly. When she leaned against his solid support, Breed brought her close, holding her to his chest.

Soon the comfort of his arms lured her back to sleep. When she woke again, Elizabeth discovered that they had both fallen asleep while sitting upright. Breed's arm remained draped around her, and he rested his head against the back of the sofa. His breathing was deep and undisturbed.

Even from a sitting position, waking up in Breed's arms felt right. She pressed her face against the side of his neck and kissed him, enjoying the light taste of salt and musk.

"Are you pretending to be Sleeping Beauty kissing awake the handsome Prince?" Breed asked opening one eye to study her.

Elizabeth barely allowed his sideways glance to touch her before straightening. "You've got that tale confused. It was the Prince who kissed Sleeping Beauty awake."

"Would it hurt you if I did?" The teasing left Breed's voice as he brought her closer within the protective circle of his arms.

Her eyes sought his. "You could never hurt me," she said in a whisper that sounded as solemn as a vow.

"I don't ever want to," he murmured just as his lips claimed hers. The kiss was gentle and sweet. His mouth barely touched hers, enhancing the sensuality of his kiss. His hands framed her face, and he treated her as if he were handling a rare and exotic orchid.

"You're looking much more chipper this morning," Gilly said, standing in the doorway of her bedroom. She raised her hands high above her head and yawned.

"I feel a whole lot better."

"I'm happy to hear that. I don't mind telling you that you had me worried."

"You?" Breed inhaled harshly. "I don't think I've ever come closer to wanting to kill a man. It's a good thing you didn't tell who did this last night, Beth. I wouldn't have been responsible for my actions."

Elizabeth lowered her gaze to the hands folded primly in her lap. "I think I already knew that."

"Take the day off," Gilly insisted as she sauntered into the kitchen and put on water for instant coffee.

"I can't do that," Elizabeth objected strenuously. "You need me."

"I'll make do," Gilly returned confidently. She opened the refrigerator, took out a pitcher of orange juice, and poured herself a small glass. "But only for today."

Elizabeth returned to her bedroom to change clothes. When she studied herself in the mirror she found that there was no outward mark from her experiences, but the mirror couldn't reveal the inner agony of what Charlie had tried to do.

"I don't believe it," she grumbled as she walked into the living room. "Last night I wanted to die, and today I feel like the luckiest woman alive to have you two as my friends."

"We're the lucky ones," Gilly said sincerely.

"But I acted like such a fool. I can't imagine what you thought."

"You were more shocked than anything," Breed inserted with a note of confidence. "A combination of shock and pain often exaggerates the messages transmitted to the brain."

"A Mr. Know-It-All," Gilly complained, running a brush through her short, bouncy curls. "Why do you put up with him?" She directed her question to Elizabeth with a mischievous gleam.

Elizabeth shrugged and shook her head. "I don't know. But he's kinda cute."

"I amuse you, is that it?" Breed joined in the teasing banter.

"You're amusing, but not always correct," Elizabeth remarked jokingly. "The brain doesn't confuse messages of pain and shock. But I'll admit, you had me going there for a minute."

Breed had the grace to look faintly embarrassed. "Well, it sounded good at the time."

Gilly paused on her way out the door. "Have a good day, you two. Call if you need anything. And"—she hesitated and lowered her gaze—"don't hold up dinner for me."

"Working late?" Elizabeth quizzed, experiencing a twinge of guilt that her friend would be stuck at the café alone.

Gilly shook her head. "Peter said he'd be coming by, and I don't want to be here when he does."

"Honestly, Gilly, you're acting like a child."

"Maybe." Gilly didn't argue. "But at least I've got my pride."

Breed murmured something about pride doing little to keep her warm at night, but obviously didn't mean for Gilly to hear his comment.

The door clicked, indicating Gilly had left for work.

"Are you hungry?" Breed asked as he walked across the living room, his hands buried deep inside his pants' pockets.

She hadn't eaten much of her dinner the previous night, but discovered she really didn't have an appetite. "Not really."

"What you need is something scintillating to tempt you."

Wickedly batting her eyelashes, Elizabeth glanced at him and softly said, "My dear Mr. Breed, what exactly do you have in mind?"

Either Breed hadn't heard her or chose to ignore the comment.

"I think I'll go over to my place to shower and change clothes. When I come back, I'll bring us breakfast."

Her mouth dropped in mute surprise. She didn't like being ignored and, selfishly, she didn't want Breed to leave her alone. Not now. "I'll come with you," she suggested eagerly. "And while you're in the shower, I'll cook us breakfast."

His bland expression revealed his lack of enthusiasm for her suggestion. "Not this time."

Elizabeth bristled. "Why not?" The memory of her last visit to his apartment remained vivid. She hadn't been imagining things. He really didn't want her there. And yet, she couldn't imagine a reason why.

"You need extra rest."

Her eyes widened in bewildered protest.

"I was thinking that when I'm gone you could get an hour's extra sleep."

Sleep! She was dressed and had downed a cup of strong coffee. Breed didn't honestly expect her to go back to bed, did he?

"I won't be long," he told her, and without a backward glance he hurried out the door.

"Don't worry about breakfast. I'll have something ready when you come back," she called after him. Elizabeth didn't like it, but there wasn't much she could do. The impulse to speak her mind died on her lips. Now wasn't the time to confront Breed with petty suspicions about her cool welcome at his apartment.

With the cookbook resting on the kitchen counter, she skimmed over the recipe for blueberry muffins.

For the moment, keeping busy was paramount. When she stopped to think, too many dark images crowded her thoughts. For a time last night, she had started to believe Charlie's vindictive words. The fear that she was somehow responsible for her mother's death would haunt her most of her life. When a tear squeezed past her determination not to cry, Elizabeth wiped it aside angrily and forced herself to concentrate on the recipe. Rehashing the details only confused her, and she soundly rejected any more introspection on the subject.

As promised, Breed returned less than an hour later. Elizabeth let him in and locked the door.

A hand on each of her shoulders, he kissed her lightly on the cheek. He looked a million times better, his hair still wet from his shower.

"Hmmm...something smells good."

"I baked some muffins," Elizabeth mentioned as she led the way into the kitchen. Her culinary efforts were cooling on a rack on top of the counter. "I don't know how they taste. The cookbook said they were great to take along camping."

"Are you thinking of taking me into the woods and ravaging my body?" Breed joked as he lifted one from the cooling rack. Burning his fingers, he gingerly tossed it in the air several times until Elizabeth, laughing, handed him a plate.

"You might have told me they were still hot."

"And miss viewing those acrobatics? Never." Her mood had lightened with Breed's. Sitting beside him at the circular table, Elizabeth peeled an orange and popped a section into her mouth. Breed smiled at her with a look of carefree abandon.

"How about a trip to our beach today?" he suggested, and his masculine mouth curved into a sensuous smile.

"Sure." Her glance caught sight of his massive hands. A slight swelling in one of the knuckles captured her attention. Had Breed been fighting? Showering hadn't taken him an hour. Immediately the thought flashed through her mind that he'd gone to her brother. "Breed." Her eyes sought his as she swallowed at the thickness lodged in her throat. "Give me your hand."

The teasing glitter didn't leave his eyes, and he didn't seem to notice the serious light in hers. "Is this a proposal of marriage?"

"Let me see your hand," she repeated, a throbbing lilt in her voice.

Breed went completely still. "Why?"

"Because I need to know that you didn't do anything...dumb."

He smiled briefly and pushed his chair away from the table. Standing, he walked to the other side of the room and folded his arms across his massive chest. Expelling a mirthful breath, he replied. "I didn't, although the temptation was strong. While I live, no man will ever do that to you again."

"How'd...how did you know it was Charlie..." She let the rest of the words fade.

Breed's eyes became hard points of steel. "Both you and Gilly mentioned that you had dinner with your brother last night."

"I appreciate the chivalry," Elizabeth stated evenly, "but I wish you hadn't."

"I found it more than necessary." The hard set of his features revealed the tight hold he had on his temper and his emotions.

The delicate control she had on her composure cracked. "I'm not defending him..."

"I should hope not." Breed shook his head grimly.

"But I didn't want you involved," she said.

"I'm involved already."

Elizabeth stood and, with her arms folded around her narrow waist, she paced the kitchen. The room was filled with Breed. His presence loomed in every corner. "Please understand, I don't want to argue with you."

His eyes narrowed as he moved into the other room and sat on the arm of the sofa. "I've never met anyone like you, Beth. Those two deserve to have the hell kicked out of them." He didn't mean it as a compliment.

"He's my brother," she cried defensively. "He may not be a prince of a fellow, but he's the only one I've got."

He moved into the living room, his back to her. When he turned a few minutes later, his grim look had vanished. "Are we going to the beach or not?"

Numbly, she nodded.

"Good." Long strides crossed the distance separating them. Breed took her by the shoulders and sweetly kissed her. "Let's hurry. It's isn't every day that I get you all to myself."

They rode in his Peugeot, and again Elizabeth wondered why Breed no longer drove Hilda. Maybe the Jeep needed repairs and he couldn't afford to have them done until his finances improved. Elizabeth wished there was some way she could do those types of things for Breed without his knowing. Offering him money wasn't the answer; it was a sure way of crushing his fragile male ego. What was the use of having money if she couldn't spend it the way she wanted?

The surf rolled gently against their bare feet as they strolled along the smooth beach, their arms entwined.

"Tell my about your childhood," Breed mused on a curious note after a lengthy, companionable silence.

Under other circumstances Elizabeth may have had the courage to reveal her wealth. But not today. She'd faced enough upheaval in the last twenty-four hours to warrant caution. The line of her mouth tightened with tension before she managed to speak.

"What's there to tell? I was born, grew up, went to school, graduated, went to school some more, dropped out, and traveled a little."

"Nicely condensed, I'd say."

"Have you been to Europe?" She hoped to deftly change the subject.

"No, but I spent six months in New Zealand a few years back." His response told her he knew exactly what she was doing.

"Did you enjoy it?" Relieved, Elizabeth continued the game.

"I'd say it was the most beautiful country on earth, but I haven't done enough traveling to compare it with the rest of the world."

Elizabeth recalled her own trip to the South Pacific. Her time in New Zealand had been short, but she'd shared his feelings about the island nation.

"My mother used to love to travel," Elizabeth commented, mentally recalling the many trips they'd taken together.

"How long has she been gone?" Breed asked, his hand reaching for hers.

Elizabeth swallowed with difficulty and forced her chin up as if she were about to take a defensive stance. "She died two years ago," she explained softly through constricted throat muscles. "Even after all this time, I miss her."

Breed paused and traced a finger over her jaw and down her neck. "I'm sorry, Beth. You must have loved her very much."

"I did," she whispered on a weak note.

"Did your family do much camping?" The question came out of the blue and was obviously meant to change the mood.

"No." She had never slept in a tent in her life. Back-to-nature pursuits had never been among her father's strong interests.

"Would you like to sometime?" His gaze touched her questioning face.

"Us?"

"I was thinking of inviting Gilly along." Gently, his hand closed over hers. "And Peter," he added in afterthought.

"Peter!" Elizabeth explained. "You devious little devil."

"Of course, that will take some fancy finagling," Breed admitted.

"Fancy finagling or downright deception?"

"Deception," Breed returned immediately.

"You shock me, Andrew Breed. I wouldn't have guessed that you had a sneaky bone in your body."

His gaze slid past her to the rolling waves that broke against the compact sand. "I fear a lot of things about me would shock you," he murmured, and Elizabeth's thoughts echoed his.

"What really irritates me," Gilly continued on her tirade as she hauled another box of cooking utensils out from the kitchen, "is the fact that Peter claims to have this deep undying love for me and then he doesn't show up for three days. Count 'em, Beth, three long days."

"But you slammed the door in his face."

Gilly rolled her eyes. "Well, he deserved it."

"My goodness, Gilly, all he did was laugh."

"It's my belief that people don't laugh at someone they claim to love," Gilly shot back righteously. Hands on hips, she surveyed the living-room floor. Half of their kitchen had been packed into cardboard boxes in anticipation of the weekend camping trip. "Is that everything?"

"Well, I certainly hope so." Elizabeth couldn't believe that people actually went through all this work just for a couple of days of traipsing around the woods.

When Breed arrived he looked incredulously at the accumulated gear.

"Before you complain, I only packed what was on your list." Elizabeth flashed him an eager smile. She was ready for this new adventure, although she suffered a few qualms about not telling Gilly that Peter had been invited. Peter had left the night before and claimed a space for them in the Samuel P. Taylor State Park, north of the city.

"Well, maybe we packed a few things not on your meager list," Gilly amended. "I found that you left off several things we might need."

"I don't know how Hilda's going to carry all this food," Breed mumbled under his breath.

"Hilda," Elizabeth cried happily. "We're taking Hilda?" Before Breed could stop her, Elizabeth rushed down the stairs to the outdated Jeep parked at the curb. Gingerly she climbed into the front seat and patted the dashboard. "It's good to see you again, old girl," Elizabeth murmured affectionately.

"Will someone kindly tell me what's going on?" Gilly stood, one hand placed on her hip as she glared curiously at her friend.

"It's a long story," Breed murmured, lifting the first box on board.

Admittedly it was a tight squeeze, but they managed to bring everything the women had deemed necessary.

The radio blared, and all three were singing joyfully as they traveled. When the news came on, they paused to listen. From her precarious position in the backseat, Gilly leaned forward. "Hey, Breed, I don't see any tent back here."

"There isn't one," Breed said with a smile, glancing at Elizabeth.

"I thought we were going camping?"

"We are," Breed confirmed.

"With no tent?"

Elizabeth didn't want to carry this game any further. "Peter pitched the tent yesterday."

"Peter!" Gilly exploded. "You didn't say anything about Peter coming on this so-called trip."

Elizabeth turned and faced her friend. "Are you mad?"

Gilly's gaze raked Elizabeth's worried face. Folding her arms, she resolutely stared out the window. "Why should I be mad? My best friend in the world has just turned traitor."

"If I'm your best friend, then you have to believe I wouldn't do anything to hurt you," Elizabeth returned with quiet logic.

"I'm not answering that."

"Because I'm right," Elizabeth argued irrefutably.

"Peter loves you," Breed inserted, matching Gilly's clipped tones. "And if it means kidnapping you so that Peter has the chance to explain himself, then I don't consider that much of a crime."

"I suppose you think that someday I'll thank you for this."

"I want to be the maid of honor," Elizabeth said with a romantic sigh.

Gilly ignored her and sat in stony silence until Breed turned off the highway and entered the campgrounds. Peter had left word at the ranger station, and within a matter of minutes they were at the campsite.

"I hope you realize that I don't appreciate this one bit," Gilly said with clenched teeth.

"I believe we got the picture." Breed's mouth moved with a humorous smile.

"Really, Gilly, it won't be so bad. All we want is for you to give the poor guy a chance."

Gilly ignored her friend and turned her attention to Breed. "Did you know Beth once called you Tarzan?" she informed him saucily.

"Tarzan? Breed's large eyes rounded indignantly, and he turned to Elizabeth with a feigned look of outrage. "Beth, you didn't."

She forced herself to smile and nodded regretfully.

"In that case, will you be my Jane?"

"Love to," Elizabeth returned happily, placing her hand in his.

Peter was outside the tent and had a small fire going when Breed parked the Jeep. Breed and Elizabeth climbed out of the front seat and stretched their arms. Gilly remained inside, her arms folded as she stared defiantly ahead.

"Hi, Gilly," Peter said as he strolled up to the Jeep, his hands buried in his pockets.

Silence. Peter continued:

"I've always been one to lay my cards on the table. So damnit, you're going to listen to me. There's no place to run now."

Silence. He went on:

"You once told me that you loved me. Believe me, I'm beginning to have my doubts about that." He levered himself so that he was in the driver's seat and placed his hands on the steering wheel. "I was so shocked at your announcement that I must have said and done the worst possible things." He hesitated slightly. "The thing was, I had no idea how you felt."

"Your reaction told me that." Gilly spoke for the first time, her words tight and low.

"You see, I'd realized earlier how much you'd come to mean to me. I'd been trying to work up enough nerve to tell you my feelings had changed."

"Don't you dare lie to me, Peter...."

"I'm not," Peter returned harshly. "For two weeks I've had doors shut in my face, phones slammed in my ear. I've about had it, Gillian Haggith. I want you to marry me, and I want your answer right now."

Feeling like an intruder, Elizabeth leaned against the picnic table with Breed at her side. Fascinated, she watched as Gilly's mouth opened and closed incredulously. For the first time in recent history, Gilly was utterly speechless.

Peter's fingers tightened around the steering wheel. "Maybe this will help you decide," he mumbled, withdrawing a small diamond ring from his jeans pocket.

"Oh, Peter," Gilly cried, and she threw her arms around him as she burst into happy tears.

Chapter Eight

Shall we give the lovebirds some time alone?'' Breed whispered in Elizabeth's ear.

Elizabeth's nod was indulgent. ''How about giving me a grand tour of the grounds.''

''Love to.''

''I'm especially interested in the modern technological advances.''

His thoughtful gaze swept over her face. ''Beth, we're in the woods. There are no technological wonders out here.''

''I was thinking of things that went flush in the night.''

''Ahh, those.'' The edges of his mouth twitched briefly upward. ''Allow me to lead the way.''

Breed set a comfortable pace as they wandered around the campgrounds, taking their time. The sky couldn't have been any bluer and the air was filled with the scent of pine and evergreen. A creek bubbled cheerfully down its meandering course, and they paused for a few quiet moments of peaceful introspection. Elizabeth's thoughts drifted to her father. Their showcase home in Boston with all its splendor couldn't compare to the tranquil beauty of this forest. If he could see this place, she was confident, he would experience the serenity that had touched her in so brief a time.

Gilly had lunch cooking by the time Breed and Elizabeth returned. With an efficiency Elizabeth hardly recognized in her friend, she watched as Gilly set out the paper plates, a pan of hot beans, freshly made potato salad, and grilled hot dogs with toasted buns. The luncheon buffet was on the table for everyone to help themselves.

"I'll do the dishes," Elizabeth joked as she filled her paper plate. Gilly sat beside Elizabeth at the picnic table.

"I'm sorry about what I said earlier," Gilly murmured as telltale color crept up her neck. "It was childish and immature of me to tell Breed that you once referred to him as Tarzan." She released her breath with a thin edge of exasperation. "Actually, it was probably the stupidest thing I've ever done in my entire life. How petty can I get?"

"You had a right to be angry." Elizabeth appreciated her friend's apology. "Not telling you that Peter was coming here was underhanded and conniving."

Breed lifted his index finger. "And my idea. I take credit."

Elizabeth's eyes captured his and her gaze wavered slightly under his potent spell. "But if it had backfired, the blame would have been mine. I'm learning a lot about the workings of the male mind."

"Do you have to sit across the table from me, woman?" Peter complained as he climbed over the seat and settled next to Breed.

I'll be sitting next to you for the rest of my life," Gilly returned with a fervent, happy note. "Besides, at this angle you can feast upon my unspoiled beauty."

The diamond ring had been placed on her finger and sparkled almost as brightly as the happiness in Gilly's eyes. Things couldn't have worked out better. Elizabeth realized how miserable her friend had been the last few days and felt oddly guilty that she had been so involved in problems of her own.

"Do you two have an announcement to make?" Breed asked as he stared pointedly at Gilly's left hand.

"Gilly and I are getting married," Peter informed them cheerfully.

"No date's been set yet," Gilly inserted. "Peter thought we should talk to my parents first. And my church has a counseling class for engaged couples. I thought we should take it. And knowing my mother, she'll want a big wedding with a dinner reception afterward. So the earliest we could set the date would be autumn. Maybe early November."

"I was hoping for a quiet wedding on the beach just before dawn with our parents and close friends. Preferably next month sometime."

"Next month," Gilly choked. "We can't do that. My mother would never forgive me."

"I thought it was me you were marrying, not your mother," grumbled Peter.

Setting the palms of her hands on the tabletop, Gilly half rose from her seat and glared openly at Peter. "Are you trying to pick a fight, buster?" she asked with a saucy grin.

"Well I don't plan on acquiring a harem. It's my wedding too," Peter challenged. "I think in the interest of fairness to your future husband you should consider my ideas."

Gilly mumbled something under her breath, and reached for the potato salad.

Holding back a smile, Elizabeth glanced at Breed, who seemed to be enjoying the humor of the moment. His looks echoed her thoughts; Gilly and Peter fought much more now that they were in love.

They finished their meal in a spirited debate on the subject of man and his environment.

"I'll unload Hilda," Breed said as he finished his lunch and climbed over the picnic bench.

"I'll help," Peter offered, pointing to Gilly. "The wedding will be next month, on the beach at sunrise."

"Thanks for the invitation, big shot. I hope I can make it."

"I'm doing the dishes," Elizabeth reminded them, and she hurriedly swallowed the last bite of her meal. Everyone was suddenly busy, and she didn't want to sit idle.

The paper plates were easily disposed of in a garbage container. She placed the potato salad and leftovers in the cooler. The only items left were the plastic forks and a single saucepan.

With a dish towel draped around her neck, and the silverware, liquid soap, and rag dumped inside the saucepan, Elizabeth headed toward the creek she'd discovered with Breed.

"Hey, where are you going?" Gilly called out as Elizabeth left camp.

"To wash these." She held up the kettle. "I'll be right back. Breed said something about taking a hike."

Gilly's smile was crooked. "Yes, but I think he was referring to me and Peter. If we don't quit fighting, I have the feeling we may have to walk home."

Elizabeth located the stream without a problem and knelt on the soft earth beside the water, humming as she rubbed the rag along the inside of the aluminum pan. Out of the corner of her eye a flash of color caught her attention, and she glanced upward. A deer was poised in a meadow on the other side of the water. Mesmerized, Elizabeth watched the wild creature with a powerful sense of awe and appreciation.

Slowly, she straightened, afraid her movement would frighten off the lovely tan creature. The doe raised its regal head and Elizabeth stared into round, beautiful, dark eyes. The animal didn't appear to be frightened by her presence.

Wondering how close she could get, Elizabeth crossed the slow-moving water, stepping carefully from one stone to another. When she reached the other side, the doe was gone. Disappointed, Elizabeth walked to the site where she'd first discovered the animal. The deer had gone farther into the forest and was barely visible. Elizabeth decided to follow it, thinking she might be able to catch a glimpse of a fawn. She wished she'd thought to bring her camera. But she hadn't expected to see anything like this.

Keeping a safe distance, Elizabeth followed the deer, rather proud of her ability to track it. She realized that the animal wasn't trying to escape or there wouldn't have been a chance of following it this far.

The lovely creature paused, and Elizabeth took the opportunity to rest on a felled tree while keeping an eye on the deer. A glance at her watch told her that she'd been away from camp almost an hour. Oh, heavens, she didn't want to worry anyone. The game was fun, but she would be forced to abandon it. With bittersweet regret, Elizabeth stood and gave a waving salute to her beautiful friend.

An hour later, Elizabeth owned up to the fact that she was lost. The taste of panic filled her mouth, and she took in several breaths to calm herself.

"Help," she screamed as loudly as she could. Her voice echoed through the silent forest. "I'm here," she cried out, a frantic edge to her words. Hurrying now, she half ran through the thick woods until she stumbled and caught herself against a bush. A thorny limb caught on the flesh of her upper arm and lightly gouged her skin until a trickle of blood ran down her arm.

Elizabeth yelped with pain and grabbed at her wound. When her fingers came away sticky with blood, a sickening sensation attacked her stomach.

"Calm down," she told herself out loud, thinking the sound of her own voice would have a soothing effect. It didn't, and she paused again to force herself to breathe evenly.

"Breed, oh Breed," she whimpered as she moved through the dense cover, holding her arm. "Please find me. Please, please find me."

Her legs felt weak, and her lungs burned with the effort to push on. Every step cost her more than the previous one.

Elizabeth tried to force the terror from her mind and concentrate on happy thoughts. The memory of her mother's laughter took the edge of exertion from her steps. The long walks with Breed along the beach. She recalled their first argument and how she'd insisted that she could find the way back. Without Breed she would have been lost then. His words from that night echoed in her tired mind. *If you're ever lost, stay in one place.* Elizabeth stumbled to an abrupt halt. She stopped and looked around her. Nothing was familiar. She could be going in the opposite direction of the campgrounds for all she knew. She was dreadfully tired and growing weaker every minute, her endurance level lowered with each step.

If she was going to stop, Elizabeth decided, she would find a place where she could sit and rest. She found a patch of moss that grew beside a tree and lowered herself to a sitting position. Her breath was uneven and ragged, but she suspected it was more from fear than anything.

Someone would find her soon, she told herself. Soon. The word repeated in her mind a thousand times, offering hope.

No one could have done anything more stupid than to follow a deer like that and not mark a trail back.

Every minute seemed an hour and every hour a month as she sat and waited. When the sun began to set, Elizabeth realized she would probably be spending the night in the woods. The thought couldn't frighten her any more than she was already. At least not until darkness settled over the forest.

Not once did she doze or even try to sleep, afraid she would miss a light or the sound of a voice. Tears filled her eyes at the darkest part of the night that preceded dawn. She could die out here. Death didn't frighten her; her mother had taught her that death could sometimes be a friend. The lesson had been well learned. And just on the other side of life, Elizabeth was convinced her mother was waiting for her.

Of course, there were regrets—lots of them, things she had wanted to do in her lifetime. But most important was that she had never told Breed how much she loved him. Somehow in all the times they'd been together, all the experiences they'd shared, Elizabeth had never told him of her love.

She stood when the sun came over the horizon, its golden rays bathing the earth with its warmth. And she was so cold. For a time, in the blackest part of the night, Elizabeth had been convinced she'd freeze. Her teeth had chattered and she'd huddled into a tight ball, believing this night would be her last.

Her stomach growled and her tongue had grown thick with the need for water. For a long time she debated whether she should strike out again and look for something to drink or stay where she was. Every muscle protested when she decided to search out water, and she quickly sat back down, amazed at how weak she had become.

She tried to call out, but her voice refused to cooperate and the attempt to shout took more energy than she could muster.

With her eyes closed, her back supported by the tree trunk, Elizabeth strained her ears for the slightest sound. The day before, while walking with Breed, she had thought the woods were quiet and serene. Now she was astonished at the cacophony of sound that surrounded her. The loud squawk of birds and the rustle of branches in the breeze filled the forest. There were other noises she couldn't identify.

"Beth." Her name echoed from some faraway distance, barely discernible.

With a reserve of energy she didn't know she possessed, Elizabeth leaped to her feet and screamed back. "Here...I'm here." Certain they would never hear her feeble cry, she ran frantically toward the sound of the voice, crying as she pushed branches out of her way. They would search in another area if she couldn't make herself heard. She couldn't bear it if she had come so close to being found.

"Here," she cried again and again until her voice was hardly more than a whisper.

Breed saw her before she did him. "Thank God," he said, and the sound of it reached her. She turned and saw the torment leave his face as giant strides covered the distance between them.

Fiercely, she was hauled into his arms as Breed buried his face in her neck. A shudder ran through him as Elizabeth wrapped her arms around his neck and started to weep with relief. Huge tears of happiness rolled down her face, making wet tracks in the dust that had settled on her cheeks. She was so relieved that she didn't notice the men with Breed until he released her.

Some of the previous agony returned to Breed's eyes as he ran his finger down the dried blood that had crusted on her upper arm.

A forest ranger handed her a canteen of water and told her to take small sips. Another man spoke into a walkie-talkie, advising the members of the search party that Elizabeth had been found and was safe.

The trip back into camp was hazy in Elizabeth's memory. Questions came at her from every direction. She answered them as best she could and apologized profusely for all the trouble she had caused.

The only thing that stood out in her mind was how far she had wandered. It seemed hours before they returned to the campgrounds. Breed took over at that point, taking her in his arms and carrying her into the tent.

The next thing Elizabeth knew, she was awake and darkness surrounded her. She sat up and glanced around. Gilly lay sleeping on one side of her and Breed was on the other. Peter was beside Gilly.

Breed's eyes opened, and he sat up with her. "How do you feel?" he whispered.

"A whole lot better. Is there anything to eat? I'm starved."

He took her hand and helped her out of the sleeping bag. Sitting her at the picnic table, he rummaged around in Gilly's disorganized boxes and returned with a plate heaped with food.

Breed took the seat across the table from her, to gaze upon her unspoiled beauty, he told her. A lantern that hung from a tree dimly lit up the area surrounding the tent and table. His features were bloodless, so pale that Elizabeth felt a surge of emotion at her thoughtlessness.

She set her fork aside. "Breed, I'm so sorry. Can you forgive me?"

He wiped a hand across his face and didn't answer immediately. "I've never been so happy to see freckles in my life."

"You look terrible."

He answered her with a weak smile. "You're a brave woman, Beth. A lot of people would have panicked."

"Don't think I didn't," she told him on a shaky laugh. "There were a few hours there last night when I was sure that I'd die in those woods." She glanced lovingly at him. "The craziest part of it was that I kept thinking of all the things I regret not having done in my life."

"I suppose that's only natural."

"Do you want to know what I regretted the most?"

"What?" he asked with a tired sigh, supporting his forehead with the palms of his hands, not looking at her.

"I kept thinking how sorry I was that I'd never told you how much I love you."

Slowly, Breed raised his gaze to hers. The look in the tired amber eyes became brilliant as he studied her.

Elizabeth bit the corner of her mouth. "Well, say something," she pleaded, rubbing a hand across her forehead. "I probably would have told you long ago except that I was afraid the same thing would happen to me as happened to Gilly." She paused and inhaled a deep, wobbly breath. "I know you love me in your own way, but I—"

"In my own way," Breed returned harshly. "I love you so damn much that if we hadn't found you in those woods I would have died trying." He pulled himself away from the picnic table and walked around to her. "You asked me if I can forgive you. The answer is yes. But I don't think my heart has recovered yet. We're bound to have one hell of a married life together, I can tell you. I don't think I can take many more of your adventures."

"Married life..." Elizabeth questioned achingly.

Breed didn't answer her with words, but hauled her into his arms and held on to her as if he couldn't bear to let her go.

"If this is a dream, don't wake me," she said.

"My love is no fantasy. This is reality."

"Oh, Breed," she whispered as tears of happiness clouded her eyes. She slipped her arms around his neck and pressed her face into his strong, muscular torso.

"Are we going to argue like Peter and Gilly? Or can we have a quiet ceremony with family and a few friends?"

She brushed his lips with a feather-light kiss. "Anything you say."

"My, my, you're agreeable."

Elizabeth curled tighter in his embrace. "Just promise to love me no matter what." She was thinking of what his reaction would be to her family's wealth and social position. He had a right to know, but telling him now would ruin the magic of the moment. As for not having said anything in the past, Elizabeth was pleased that she hadn't. Breed loved her for herself. Money and all that it could buy hadn't influenced his feelings. Maybe she was anticipating trouble for no reason.

His smile broadened. The radiant light in his amber eyes drew a soft glow of happiness from her. His fingers explored her neck and shoulders, holding her so close that for a moment it was impossible to breathe normally. When he moved to kiss her, Elizabeth slid her hands over his muscular chest and linked them behind his neck. Breed allowed her only small gasps of air before a new shiver of excitement stole her breath completely.

Her parted lips were trembling and swollen from his plundering kisses when Breed groaned, pulled himself away, and sat up straight. "I think the sooner we arrange the wedding, the better." He sighed. "I'd prefer a tent built for two." He ran a hand over his eyes. "And this may be old-fashioned, but I'd like to be married when we start our family."

Elizabeth knew the music in her heart would never fade. Not with this man. He didn't sound old-fashioned to her, but refreshingly wonderful.

"I'm so glad you want children." Her voice throbbed with the beat of her heart.

"A houseful at least." His husky voice betrayed the tight rein he held on his needs. "But for now I'd be content to start with a wedding ring."

"Soon," she promised.

"Tomorrow we'll go down and get the license."

"Tomorrow?" The immediacy of a wedding frightened her as his lovemaking hadn't. She wanted to get married, but she couldn't see the necessity of rushing into it.

"Maybe we should pack up and drive to Reno and be married immediately."

"No." Elizabeth didn't know why she felt so strongly about that. "I want to stand before God to make my vows, not the Last Chance Hitching Post."

She could see Breed's smile. "You're sure you want to marry me?" he said.

In response, Elizabeth rolled over and teased him with her lips. "You'll never need to doubt my love," she said, and she playfully nipped at his earlobe.

"Who would have believed you'd get lost in the woods," Gilly commented late the next night as they unpacked the camping gear in the apartment kitchen.

"Who would have believed we'd both become engaged in one weekend."

"Elizabeth, I can't tell you how frantic we all were." Gilly said tightly. "Breed was like a man possessed. When you didn't come back, he went to find you. When he didn't return, Peter and I went to look for you both."

Color heated Elizabeth's face. "I was so stupid." Her inexperience had ruined their trip. After a good night's sleep, they'd packed up and headed back to San Francisco.

"Don't be so hard on yourself. This was your first time camping. You didn't know."

"But I feel so terrible to have been such an idiot."

Gilly straightened and brushed the hair off her forehead. "I thank God you're safe," she said, staring into the distance. "I don't know what would have happened to Breed if we hadn't found you. Beth, he was like a madman. I don't think there was anyone who didn't realize that if you weren't found, Breed would die in the attempt."

Leaning against the counter, Elizabeth expelled a painful sigh. "On the bright side of things, getting lost has done a lot for Breed and me. I wonder how long it would have been before we admitted how we felt."

"It's taken too long as it is. I knew almost from the beginning that you two were meant for each other."

Elizabeth attempted to disguise a smile. "We don't all have your insight, I guess."

Gilly seemed unaware of the teasing glint in her roommate's eye. "Peter's coming over in a few minutes. We're going to talk to my parents. Will you be safe all by yourself, or should I phone Breed?"

"He's coming over in a while. I'm cooking dinner."

Breed arrived five minutes after Gilly left with Peter. He kissed her lightly on the cheek. "How do you feel?"

"Hungry," she said with a warm smile. "Let's get this show on the road."

"I thought you were cooking me dinner."

"I am. But we left the food in Hilda, at your place. If I'm going to share my life with you, then the least you can do is introduce me to your kitchen."

That uneasy look came over his features again. "We could go out just as well."

"Breed," Elizabeth intoned dramatically. "How many times do we have to argue about this apartment of yours? It's so obvious you don't want me there."

His mouth tightened grimly. "Let's go. I don't want another argument."

"Well, that's encouraging."

The brisk walk took them about fifteen minutes. Breed's apartment was exactly as she remembered it. No pictures or knickknacks that claimed the place as Breed's. This one thing continued to confuse her, but she couldn't believe that he would hide anything from her.

His cupboards were bare, but Elizabeth assumed this was because he ate most of his meals out.

"Spaghetti's my specialty," she told him as she tied an apron around her waist.

"That sounds good."

He hovered at her elbow as she fried the meat and stood at her side while she chopped the vegetables. Breed guarded every action she made, and when she couldn't tolerate his brand of "togetherness" another second, she turned and ushered him into the living room.

"Read the paper or something, will you? You're driving me crazy."

Breed's eyes showed indecision. He glanced back into the kitchen, then nodded as he reached for the newspaper.

Singing softly as she worked, Elizabeth mentally reviewed her cooking lessons from school. The sauce was simmering and the noodles were boiling. She decided to set the table. A few loose papers and mail littered the countertop. Humming cheerfully, she delivered it to his desk on the far side of the kitchen. The top of the desk was cluttered with papers. As she set down his mail, Elizabeth noticed a legal-looking piece of paper. She continued to hum as idly she glanced over its content. A gun permit. Breed carried a gun. A chill shot up her spine. The song died on her lips. She had always thought of him as a gentle giant. Breed and firearms seemed as incongruous as mixing oil and water. She'd ask him about it later.

"Anything I can do?" Breed volunteered, seeming to have relaxed now.

"Open the wine."

"Wine?"

"You mean you don't have any?" Elizabeth asked as she stirred the noodles. "The flavors in my sauce will be incomplete without the complement of wine."

"I take it you want me to buy us a bottle."

"You got it."

"Okay, let's go." He stood and tucked in his shirttails.

"Me? I can't go now. I've got to drain the noodles and finish setting the table."

Breed hesitated.

"Honestly, Breed, there's a grocery just down the street. You don't need me to hold your hand."

He didn't look pleased about it, but he turned and walked out.

The minute the door was closed, Elizabeth returned to his desk. She felt like she was snooping, but the gun permit puzzled her and she wanted to look it over. The permit listed a different address, confirming her suspicions that he hadn't been in this apartment long. The paper felt like it was burning her fingers, and she set it aside, hating the way her curiosity had gotten in the way of her better judgment.

She could ask him, of course, but she felt uneasy about that. Where would he keep a lethal weapon in this bare place? She wondered about the kind of gun he carried. With her index finger she pulled out the top desk drawer. It wasn't in sight, but a book with her full name written across the top riveted her gaze. Fascinated, Elizabeth pulled it from the drawer and flipped it open. Pagc after page of meticulous notes detailed her comings and goings, her habits and her friends. *Breed had been following her since she arrived!* But whatever for? Questions about his actions had troubled her in the past, but this was bizarre.

Coiled tightness gripped her throat as she pulled open another drawer. Hurt and anger and a thousand terrifying emotions she had never thought to experience with Breed filled her senses. The drawer was filled with correspondence with her father. Andrew Breed had been hired by her family as her bodyguard.

Chapter Nine

Elizabeth backed away from the drawer. Her hand was pressed against her breast as the blood drained from her face. Her heart was pounding wildly in her ears, and for several seconds she was unable to breathe. So many inconsistencies about Breed fell into place. Elizabeth was amazed that she could have been so blind, and so utterly stupid. His cover had been perfect. Dating her had simplified his job immeasurably.

Her stomach buckled, and Elizabeth knew she was going to be sick. She closed the drawer and staggered into the bathroom. It was there that Breed found her.

"Beth." His voice was filled with concern. "You look terrible."

She didn't meet his eyes. "I'm...I'm all right. I just need a moment."

He placed his arm across her back, and the touch, although light, seemed to burn through the material of her shirt, branding her. Leading her into the living room, Breed sat her down on the sofa and brought in a cool rag.

"I was afraid something like this might happen," he murmured solicitously. "You're probably having a delayed reaction to the trauma of this weekend."

Elizabeth closed her eyes and nodded, still unable to look at him. "I want to go home." Somehow the words managed to slip past the strangulation hold she felt against her throat.

Not until they were ready to leave did Elizabeth glance out Breed's window and note that her apartment could be seen from his. She'd never thought about the close proximity of their buildings. Although it was a number of blocks' walking distance, the two apartment houses were within easy sight of one another. No wonder he was able to document her whereabouts so accurately. Mr. Andrew Breed was a clever man, deceptive and more devious than she could have dreamed. And he excelled at his job. Elizabeth didn't try to fool herself; she was a job to him and probably little or nothing more than that.

It was no small wonder he'd suggested they go to Reno and get married right away. He wanted the deed accomplished before they confronted her father. Breed knew what her family would say if she were to marry a bodyguard. The emotions she'd experienced when her purse had been taken were similar to what she felt now. A part of her inner self had been violated. But the pain went far deeper. Deep enough to sear her soul. Elizabeth doubted that she'd ever be the same again.

Concerned, Breed helped her on with her sweater and gripped her elbow. Several times during the short drive to her apartment he glanced her way, a worried look marring his handsome face. After he had unlocked her apartment and helped her into her bedroom, Elizabeth changed clothes, took a sleeping pill, and climbed into bed. But the pill didn't work. She lay awake with a lump the size of a grapefruit blocking her throat. Every swallow grated against her larynx. Crying would help, but no tears would come.

Elizabeth didn't know how long she lay staring at the shadows on the ceiling. The front door clicked open, and she heard Breed whisper to Gilly. Elizabeth was mildly surprised that he'd stayed, then grinned sarcastically. Of course he would; he'd been paid to baby-sit her. And knowing her father, the fee had been generous.

The front door clicked again, and she heard Gilly assure Breed that she would take care of Elizabeth. The words were almost ludicrous. These two people whom she'd come to love this summer had given her so much. But they had taken away even more. No, she didn't blame Gilly. Elizabeth was grateful to have had her as a friend. Gilly may have been in on this scheme, but she doubted it.

The room grew dark, and Elizabeth heard Gilly go into her bedroom. An hour later, convinced Gilly would be asleep, Elizabeth silently laid back the covers and climbed out of bed. Dragging the suitcases from the closet, she quickly and quietly emptied her drawers and hangers. She only took what she brought with her. Everything else she was leaving for her roommate.

The apartment key and a note to Gilly were left propped against a flower vase on the kitchen table. A sad smile touched Elizabeth's pale features as she set a second note addressed to Breed beside Gilly's. She picked it up and read over the simple message again. It read: *The game's over. You lose.*

The taxi ride to the airport seemed to take hours. Elizabeth kept looking over her shoulder, afraid Breed was following. She didn't want to think of how many times this summer he had done exactly that. The thought made her more determined than ever to get away.

There wasn't a plane scheduled to leave for Boston until the next morning, so Elizabeth took the first available flight to New York. Luckily, the wait was less than two hours. Her greatest fear was that Gilly would wake up and go to check on her. Once finding her gone, Gilly would be sure to contact Breed.

Restlessly, Elizabeth walked around the modernized airport. Whatever memories remained from this summer, Elizabeth knew that she'd never forget this city. The cable cars, the sounds and smells of Fisherman's Wharf, sailing, the beach...her musings did a buzzing tailspin. No, thoughts of San Francisco would always be irrevocably tied to Breed. She wanted to hate him, but she couldn't. He'd given her happy memories and she'd struggle to keep those untainted with the mud of his deception.

The flight was uneventful. The first-class section had only one other traveler, a businessman who worked out of his briefcase the entire time.

Even though it was only ten A.M. when her plane landed, New York was sweltering in an August heat wave. The limousine delivered her to the St. Moritz, a fashionable uptown hotel that was situated across the street from Central Park South.

Exhausted to the point that she was rummy, Elizabeth took a hot shower and fell asleep almost immediately afterward in the air-conditioned room.

When she awoke, it was dinnertime. Although she hadn't eaten anything in twenty-four hours, she wasn't hungry.

A walk in Central Park lifted her from the swell of overwhelming self-pity. She bought a pretzel and squirted thick yellow mustard over it. As she lazily strolled beside the pond, goldfish the size of trout came to the water's edge, anticipating a share of her meal. Not wanting to disappoint them, she broke off a piece of the doughy pretzel and tossed it into the huge pond.

A young bearded man, strumming a ballad on his guitar, sat on a green bench looking for handouts. Elizabeth placed a five-dollar bill in the open guitar case, prompting the musician to call out.

"Thanks, lady," he sang, and he returned her wave with a bob of his dark head.

Most of the park benches were occupied with a wide range of people from all walks of life. Elizabeth had taken a two-day trip that spring to the Big Apple and stayed at the St. Moritz. But she hadn't gone into Central Park. The thought hadn't entered her mind.

Today she strolled around the pond, hoping that the sights and sounds of the vibrant city would ease the heaviness in her heart. Unfamiliar settings filled with anonymous faces were no longer intimidating. San Francisco had done that for her.

An hour later she stepped into the cool hotel room and sighed. Reaching for the phone, she dialed Boston.

"Hello, Dad," she greeted, her voice devoid of emotion.

"Elizabeth, where are you?" he demanded instantly.

"New York."

"Why in heaven's name did you run off like that?"

His question drew a faint smile. "I think you already know why," she answered softly, resignedly. "How often have you hired men to watch me in the past?"

"Did he tell you?" her father responded brusquely.

"No. I found out on my own."

"The fool," he issued harshly under his breath.

Elizabeth disagreed. The only fool in this situation had been herself for falling in love with Breed.

"I was afraid he'd do something like that."

"He didn't," Elizabeth repeated. "I found out on my own.

A strained silence stretched between the wires.

"How often, Dad?"

"Only a few," he answered after a long moment.

"But why?" she asked, exhaling forcefully. The pain of this knowledge was physical as well as mental. Her stomach ached and she lowered herself into the upholstered wing chair in her suite and leaned forward to rest her elbows on her knees.

"That's a subject we shouldn't discuss over the phone. I want you at home."

"There are a lot of things I want too," she returned in a shallow whisper.

"Elizabeth, please. Be reasonable."

"Give me a few days," she insisted. "I need time to think."

Her father began to argue. Elizabeth closed her eyes and listened for a few moments. "Good-bye, Dad," she whispered, and she hung up.

The next morning she checked out of the hotel, rented a car, and headed north. Setting a leisurely pace, she stopped along the way to enjoy the beauty of the Atlantic Ocean. It took Elizabeth three days to drive home.

She recognized that her father would consider her actions immature, but for Elizabeth, this time alone with her thoughts had been vital. The long drive, the magnificent coastline, the solitude, gave her the necessary time to come to terms with her father's actions. Decisions were made. Although her father hadn't asked for it, she gave him her forgiveness. He had been doing what he thought was best.

The thing that shocked her had been her stupidity. How could she have been so gullible? All the evidence of Breed's deceit had been there, and she had been blinded by her love. But no more. Never again. Loving someone only caused emotional pain. She had been naive and incredibly foolish.

Elizabeth wouldn't allow her father to interfere in her life like this again. Once home, she would make arrangements to find a place on her own. Breaking away had been long overdue. This summer she'd proved to her father and herself that she was capable of holding a job. And that was what Elizabeth decided to do. She spoke fluent French and enough German and Italian to make her last visit to Europe trouble-free.

Not once during the drive home did she allow bitterness to tarnish her memories of Breed. Ultimately the special relationship they'd shared led to heartache. But she was grateful to him for the precious gift that he'd so unwittingly given her.

One thing Elizabeth couldn't accept was his calculated deception. Maybe forgiveness would come later, but the pain cut so deep that it would take a long time, and maybe never.

Midafternoon Elizabeth pulled up in front of the huge family home. She didn't bother to carry any luggage inside with her. Bently would see to that.

The white-haired butler opened the door and gave her a stiff but genuine smile.

"Welcome home, Miss Elizabeth." His head dipped slightly as he spoke.

"Hello, Bently."

"Your father's been expecting you, miss. You're to go directly to the library."

Although the diplomatic old man hadn't said as much, he was warning her that her father wasn't pleased.

"I'll see to your luggage," he continued.

"Thank you, Bently."

Her elderly ally inclined his head in silent understanding.

Elizabeth stood in the great entry hall and looked round her with new eyes. The house was magnificent, a showpiece, but it felt cold and unwelcoming. The heart of this home had died with her mother.

Knocking politely against the polished mahogany door that reached from the ceiling to the floor, Elizabeth waited with calm deliberation.

Charles Wainwright's reply was curt and impatient. "Come in."

"Hello, Father," she said as she walked through the door.

"Elizabeth." He raised himself out of his chair. Relief relaxed the tightness in his weathered brow and he gave her a brief, perfunctory hug. "Now, what's all this nonsense of needing time away?"

Elizabeth was saved a reply by Helene. The maid seemed to appear noiselessly, carrying a silver tray with a coffeepot and two delicate china cups.

Both Elizabeth and her father waited to resume conversation until the girl had left the room.

"I have a few unanswered questions of my own," Elizabeth said as she stood and dutifully filled the first cup. She handed it to her father. Charles Wainwright's hair was completely white now, Elizabeth noted as he accepted the steaming cup from her hand. Once, a long time past, her father's hair had been the same sandy shade as her own. The famous Wainwright blond good looks. Charlie was dark like her mother. But other than her coloring, Elizabeth felt like she had nothing in common with this man. He wasn't affectionate. She couldn't ever recall him bouncing her on his knee or telling her stories when she was a child. The only time she recalled seeing deep emotion from him had been after her mother's funeral.

Her reverie was interrupted by coffee that dripped from the spout of the silver service and scalded her fingertips. Elizabeth managed to set the pot aside before giving an involuntary gasp of surprise. Tears filled her eyes, but not from physical pain.

"Elizabeth." Charles Wainwright leapt to his feet. "You've burned yourself." He turned aside. "Helene," he shouted. Elizabeth could never remember hearing more emotion in his voice. "Bring the first-aid kit."

"I'm fine," she struggled to reassure him between sobs. Elizabeth hadn't wept when she learned of Breed's deceit. Nor had she revealed her grief at her mother's funeral. After all, she was a Wainwright, and tears were a sign of weakness. Now she was home with possibly the only person alive who loved her for herself, and they sat like polite acquaintances, sharing coffee and shielding their hearts. A dam within her burst, and she began to sob uncontrollably.

She could see by the concerned look on his face that Charles Wainwright didn't know how to react. He raised and lowered his hands, impotently unsure of himself. Finally he circled his arms around her and patted her gently on the back as if he were afraid she was a fragile porcelain doll that would break.

"Princess," he whispered, "what is it?"

Helene burst in the door and Charles dismissed her with a wave of his hand.

"Who's hurt you?"

Between a fresh wave of sobs, she shook her head.

Her father handed her his starched and pressed linen handkerchief and Elizabeth held the cloth to her eyes.

"My dear," Charles said, smoothing her back. "You have the look of a woman in love."

"No." Elizabeth pulled free of his loose embrace and violently shook her head. "I can't love him after what he's done," she choked out between sobs.

"And what did he do?"

Elizabeth sniffled. "Nothing. I...can't talk about it. Not now," she whispered in painful denial. "I apologize for acting like a ninny. I'll go upstairs and lie down for an hour or so and be fine."

"Princess, are you sure you won't tell me?"

Fresh tears squeezed through her damp lashes. "Not now." She turned toward the great hall. "Dad," she said with her back to him, "I'll probably be leaving for Europe within the week."

Her father was silent for a moment. "Running away won't solve anything." His haunting voice, gentle with wisdom, came to her as she left the library.

One suitcase was packed and another half-filled. Elizabeth knew after one night that she couldn't remain in this house. Once the tears had come, the aching loneliness in her heart had throbbed with its intensity. Her father was right when he told her running away wouldn't heal the void. But escaping came naturally; she had been doing it for so long. Last night she hadn't gone down to dinner and was shocked when her father brought her a tray later in the evening. Elizabeth had pretended to be asleep. She regretted that now, and decided to go downstairs and say goodbye to her father.

Tucking her passport in her purse, she examined the contents of her suitcases one last time before securing the locks and leaving them outside her door. The reservations for her flight had been made earlier that morning, and plenty of time remained before she needed to leave for the airport. But already she was restless. Forcing a smile on her pale features, she descended the stairs.

Elizabeth was only midway down the winding staircase when she heard Bently engaged in a heated argument with someone at the front door. The voice of the other party was achingly familiar. Breed.

That he was angry and impatient was apparent as Breed's raised voice echoed through the hall. Elizabeth took another step, when her father appeared in the open entryway.

"That'll be all, Bently," Charles Wainwright said with calm authority. "I'll see Mr. Breed."

Elizabeth restrained a gasp and pulled closer to the banister. Apparently neither man was aware of her presence as she stood poised on the stairway.

Breed stepped into the house. His deeply tanned features were set in hard lines as he approached her father.

"I appreciate the fact that you're seeing me." Breed's voice was laced with heavy sarcasm. "But I can assure you that I was prepared to wait as long as it took."

"After four days of pounding down my door, I can believe that's a fair assumption," Mr. Wainwright retorted stiffly. "But now that you have my attention, what is it you want?"

"Elizabeth," Breed said without hesitation. "Where is she?"

"Your job of protecting my daughter was terminated when she left San Francisco. I believe you've received your check."

Elizabeth watched, fascinated and shocked as Breed took the envelope from his pocket and ripped it in two. "I don't want a dime of this money. I told you that before, and I'm telling you again."

"You earned it."

Every damn penny, Elizabeth wanted to shout at him.

"I kept my word, Wainwright," Breed explained forcefully. "I didn't tell Beth a thing. But I hated every minute of this assignment, and you knew it."

"Why? I thought this type of work was your specialty. You came highly recommended," Mr. Wainwright said quietly.

Breed rubbed a hand across his eyes, and the torment Elizabeth saw in his features was mirrored in her own. When he lowered his hand, he must have caught a glimpse of her from out of the corner of his eye. He hesitated and turned toward her.

"Beth." He said her name softly, as though he was afraid she would disappear again. He moved to the foot of the stairs. The tightness eased from his face as he stared up at her.

"Mr. Wainwright," Breed said, and the anger was gone from his voice as he glanced briefly at her father. "I love your daughter."

"No," Elizabeth cried in agitation. "You don't know the meaning of the word. I was nothing more than a lucrative business proposition."

Breed ripped another envelope from his shirt and handed it to her father. His eyes left her only briefly. "I thought you'd bring up the matter of money."

Her gaze wavered under the blazing force of his.

"This paper proves that I'm not a poor man. I own a thousand acres of California prime timberland. The land has been in my family for a hundred years," Breed stated evenly. "I haven't any need for the Wainwright money. From the first day I met your daughter, it's stood between us like a brick wall."

Breed turned back to the stairs, and his look grew gentle. "I love you, Beth Wainwright. I've loved you from the moment you went swimming and revealed your freckles for the first time."

Her heart was crying out for her to run to Breed. But the feelings of betrayal and hurt kept her rooted to the stairs. Her hand curved around the polished banister until she was sure her long fingernails would dent the wood.

At her silence, Breed returned his attention to her father. "Mr. Wainwright, I'm asking for your permission to marry your daughter—"

"I won't marry you," she interrupted in angry protest. "You lied to me. All those weeks you..."

"You weren't exactly honest with me," Breed returned levelly. "And there was ample opportunity for you to explain everything. You have no right to get indignant with me." He paused, and the hardness left his chiseled features. "Now, I'll ask you again. I love you, Beth. I want you to share my life."

Indecision played across her face, and her gaze met her father's. Breed's eyes followed hers, and a proud mask stole over him.

"I'm asking for your permission, Wainwright," Breed said coolly. "But I'll be honest; I plan to marry your daughter with or without it."

A hint of mirth touched the wrinkled face. "That's a brash statement, young man."

"Daddy," Elizabeth called, knowing what her father would say to someone like Breed. Her heart and her pride waged a desperate battle.

Charles Wainwright ignored his daughter. "As it is, I realize that Elizabeth loves you. I may be a crusty old man, but I'm not so blind to see that you'll make her happy. You have my permission, Andrew Breed. Fill this house with grandchildren and bring some laughter into its halls again."

Breed appeared as stunned as Elizabeth.

"Go on." Charles Wainwright flicked his wrist in the direction of his daughter. "And don't take no for an answer."

"I have no intention of doing so," Breed said as he climbed the stairs two at a time.

Elizabeth had the crazy desire to turn and run, but she stayed where she was, her body motionless with indecision. She bit into a trembling bottom lip as her pride surrendered the first battle.

"Your money will go into the trust fund for our children, Beth," he began with a frown. "I don't want a penny of what's yours. There's only one thing I'm after."

"What's that?" she asked in a quiet murmur, battling with the potency of his nearness.

Breed slid his hands around her waist and pulled her within the circle of his arms. "A wife."

Her breath came in small flutters as he lowered his mouth to hers and paused a scant inch above her. Their breath merged, his warm and scented. Elizabeth swayed against him, her hands moving over his chest. The entire time her pride urged her to break free and walk away. But her heart held her steadfast.

"Don't fight me so hard," he whispered, claiming her lips in a kiss that was so tender that she melted against him.

"Together we'll build a lumber kingdom," Breed whispered into her hair.

"I don't know," she faltered. "I need time to think; I'm confused." She wanted him so much, but it was her pride that was speaking, not her heart.

"Elizabeth," her father called from the hall. "I think it's only fair to tell you that your Andrew came to me a few weeks back and asked to be relieved of this case. Naturally, I declined and demanded that he maintain his anonymity."

Elizabeth's eyes met Breed's. "Your business trip?"

He nodded and placed a hand on each of her soft shoulders. "Is it really so difficult to decide?" Breed asked in a husky whisper.

Elizabeth stared at the familiar features and saw the pain carved in them. "No, not at all."

For a breathless moment they looked at one another.

Elizabeth's pride surrendered to her heart as she pressed her mouth to his.

READERS' COMMENTS ON SILHOUETTE ROMANCES:

"The best time of my day is when I put my children to bed at naptime and sit down to read a Silhouette Romance. Keep up the good work."

P.M.*, Allegan, MI

"I am very fond of the quality of your Silhouette Romances. They are so real. I have tried to read some of the other romances, but I always come back to Silhouette."

C.S., Mechanicsburg, PA

"I feel that Silhouette Books offer a wider choice and/or variety than any of the other romance books available."

R.R., Aberdeen, WA

"I have enjoyed reading Silhouette Romances for many years now. They are light and refreshing. You can always put yourself in the main characters' place, feeling alive and beautiful."

J.M.K., San Antonio, TX

"My boyfriend always teases me about Silhouette Books. He asks me, how's my love life and naturally I say terrific, but I tell him that there is always room for a little more romance from Silhouette."

F.N., Ontario, Canada

*names available on request

RCR

precious, private moments and secret dreams... experience every whispered word of love, every ardent touch, every passionate heartbeat.

As a home subscriber, you will also receive FREE, a subscription to the Silhouette Books Newsletter as long as you remain a member. Each issue is filled with news on upcoming titles, interviews with your favorite authors, even their favorite recipes.

And, the first 4 Silhouette Books are absolutely FREE and without obligation, yours to keep! What could be easier...and where else could you find such a satisfying reading experience?

To get your free books, fill out and return the coupon today!